VICE TRAP

"...hits you where you live."—*Real Magazine*

"*Vice Trap* is an unsung hard crime noir novel,
and Elliott Gilbert has given us a mini-
masterpiece of the genre!"—Gary Lovisi

Elliott Gilbert Bibliography
(1924-2000)

Crime Fiction:

Don't Push Me Around (Popular Library, 1955)
Vice Trap (Avon, 1958)
Too Much Woman (Beacon, 1961)

VICE TRAP

Elliott Gilbert

Black Gat Books • Eureka California

For Wendy

VICE TRAP

Published by Black Gat Books
A division of Stark House Press
1315 H Street
Eureka, CA 95501, USA
griffinskye3@sbcglobal.net
www.starkhousepress.com

VICE TRAP
Originally published by Avon Publications, Inc., New York, and
copyright © 1958 by Elliott Gilbert.

ISBN: 979-8-88601-136-4

Text design by Mark Shepard, shepgraphics.com
Cover design by Jeff Vorzimmer, ¡caliente!design, Austin, Texas
Cover art by Harry Schaare
Proofreading by Bill Kelly

First Stark House Press/Black Gat Edition: February 2025

ONE

Well, the three of us were there in the back, running out a hand of seven-card stud, when Louis put his head in the door.

"Friend of yours says he's outside, Nick."

"I thought you knew all my friends," I said.

"Do you have any left?" Louis grinned.

"I'll see," I told Graemie, and I pushed a quarter into the pot.

Graemie turned up the hole jack. He'd had the two of them, all right. Sand-o hadn't looked. He was out five or six dollars so far, mostly to Graemie.

I got up and went out through the front. Louis was talking to the fat beer salesman, Drucker. I saw Drucker had sprung already. The half-dozen guys standing at the bar had Lucky bottles in front of them.

Outside, this old blue Plymouth coupe was stopped down there in the bus zone. The sun was reflecting on its hazed-up back window. There was something familiar about the crate, I thought. Then I made the heavy-set guy waiting behind the wheel.

What the hell, I thought.

He was grinning, round-jawed, as I came over.

"How's hustling, hombre?" He was always pretty smart-talking, this Madrid.

"You haven't changed," I said.

"Not in two years, man. Get in the jalop. I want to talk to you."

"This is close enough for me."

"Jesus, you're still the touchy stud, aren't you?"

A Metro bus came up just then and beeped its horn.

It had a sign across the front about the concerts at the Hollywood Bowl. The driver was looking at me through the windshield. I opened the Plymouth's door and got in.

This Madrid drove through the noon-hour traffic for a couple of blocks. Then he turned into the long alley that runs in back of the Goodnight Café.

"They've got a new bunch of heads in here. I looked for you inside."

"Is that so?"

"That Louis' back there is new, too. When did old Dryman sell out?"

"Why don't you find him and ask him?" I said.

"That was a hell of a name for a gin mill anyway—Dryman's."

We came out of the alley, then turned up Marine Boulevard. After a few blocks I began to smell the ocean.

He switched on the radio.

"Nothing like a little music eh?" Everything he'd said so far made that kind of sense.

I looked at him punching the station buttons. This Madrid had graying kinky hair, a flat nose, and heavy shoulders. He had little eyes, like black olives, in his big Indian face. He would be around thirty-nine now, I thought. He was wearing a double-breasted brown pinstripe suit, the kind the Mexicans figure is the thing.

I took my cigarettes out of my shirt pocket. He pushed the dash lighter, then held it for me. He was like some head waiter all right.

"What are you doing these times, hombre?"

"I don't have to tell you."

He grinned, big-faced. "Same old Nick." He

pronounced it Nake. Another thing was the "hombre" business. I'm a Greek, myself, but I've had that word hung on me because I can speak a little Mexican, and, occasionally, I've passed for one of them.

"I've got a steady gig. If it's any of your business," I said.

"Oh? That's good. Where?"

"Carroll's Richfield. Mechanic on duty."

"You on the percentage?"

"Sure. I can give green stamps too. Anything more you'd care to know?"

"You work Sundays? This is your day off, eh?"

My knees were touching the dash. I straightened up. "Listen," I said, "Madrid. Suppose you tell me what the hell you want."

"Relax, can't you, man?" He was driving fast with one hand on the wheel.

We were on the ocean front. He drove past the strip of beach where the city has the public barbecue pits. A few of the muscle bums were out playing volleyball. Then he turned into the parking lot of the frozen freeze drive-in.

He stopped in back, near the outside toilet the fairies hang around when it's dark. He knew those places from when he was on the vice squad. That was before he'd become a narco heat.

He unbuttoned his coat and opened a pack of cigarettes. The sun was hot through the windshield, and you could get that toilet smell and the disinfectant. The radio was still playing.

"I want you to do me a favor, man. A little thing."

Well, it was pretty funny, right then. Because it was a small car inside, and the spinner was down toward me, the way he'd cut the wheel, and I could see this snapshot of Lona set into the plastic knob. I wondered if he realized it.

"Go to hell," I said.

"I know, man. But you can use a couple bucks, I bet. This's a legit deal, you know."

"Then what do you need me for?"

"Cut out talking like a loser."

"Yes?" I said. "And you wouldn't know anything about that?"

"You got yourself in that beef. You only did three months because I put a word in for you," he said.

"After you busted me. Well, you listen to me," I said. "Because maybe it has been two years, but you're still crut in my book. And now you drive back here outside the can of this custard joint, and come on with a spiel about some favor you want me to do you. Well, I wouldn't touch you with gloves."

"It's only this tape recorder, man. Just like new. I want to fence it. Hell, you know it wouldn't be hot."

I snorted on my cigarette. He wasn't funny anymore. I didn't know what he was.

"You get a fence, he'll go more than I could get for the damn thing secondhand. That's all there is to it. You can take out anything for your end."

"You don't work around here anymore. And since when didn't you know all the goniffs?"

"They wouldn't do business with me."

"But I'm supposed to."

"For a fa-vor," he singsonged it.

"That's what really gets me. Maybe you have that thing playing in here right now?"

He looked disgusted. "Why would I want to get you in trouble?"

"That's what I'm trying to figure," I said.

A guy in a white coat and apron came out of the frozen freeze. He threw some trash in a can. He stood there watching the beach.

This Madrid blew smoke through his big white teeth. "I got a couple, three bills I can't make, Nick. It's Lona's machine. She's tired of taping the jazz programs on it anyhow. So we figured we could use the dough."

He was talking with one hand, and I could see the gold band there on his finger.

He was waiting for me to ask about Lona, I knew. So I did. To show him I didn't give a damn about it anymore.

"Listen," I told him. "Go turn yourself somebody else. I'm busy."

"You still teed with me about Lona, man? That's really it, I bet you. You did that three months on your ear, sure. Hell, how long you go with her, was it?"

The stupid bastard. Well, he was, putting it like that. Because I had known Lona all this time. And I was shacking with her then, where he came in.

That was when he and the other two cops came busting into my place, and there wasn't time to eat the grass Lona and I were smoking. So I got ninety days in the County. And while I was inside this Madrid took up with her, Lona and him using plenty of maryjane. All those narco heat know where to come by the stuff, and some smoke it occasionally themselves. Anyway, they found out pretty quick he was running around with her, and that he hadn't even put her in his report. Probably one of those other two turned him in. So she married him, just after they kicked him off the force. He was just a hick cop now, I'd heard, in some town out near the edge of the desert.

I never really knew why Lona'd done it—maybe out

of some kind of pity, or obligation even. Maybe because he could score for some things, still, a lot easier than anyone else ever could for her. You can't figure a balling chick. And Lona was one before I'd turned on anything with her.

"I guess I never did think about asking her to marry me," I said to him.

"Sure. That's right."

"Me and a whole bunch of other studs."

He laid his arm across the top of the seat. His coat fell open and I could see the butt of the off-duty .32 he was wearing inside his belt. You give a Mexican a watchman's badge even, and he goes around bumping into doorjambs.

I thought I would try to get that .32 out of the way.

His face was drained, pasty-looking. He didn't say anything; just sitting there looking at me. He almost looked as if he was going to cry. He must have wanted to fence that tape recorder pretty bad, I thought.

"All right," I said. I threw my cigarette out the window. "Where have you got it, in the trunk?"

When I came back inside Louis', Graemie and Sand-o were gone. I figured Sand-o had run out of money the way he'd been going. I told Louis to give me a bottle of beer.

I had the tape recorder outside in my Ford. I had to hustle it that afternoon. Madrid was coming back the next day. He'd told me he worked the graveyard shift in a radio car out in this place called Cuesta. It was in the Imperial Valley; one of those jackrabbit towns you see down around the border out there.

"Who was your Mex friend?" Louis asked me, leaning on the bar.

Being Greek, I know what it's like to be spoken about that way. Sometimes Louis tried to be a little too chummy and it didn't go over. He used to run a kids' hangout malt shop before be bought this place when old Dryman got sick.

"Why didn't you say Drucker was in springing beers?" I said. "We were playing kitty cards back there, weren't we?"

"Say, I did forget, didn't I? Well, you can have this one on me, hombre, man."

"Another time," I said.

TWO

The next morning I was fooling around for twenty minutes, trying to pull the fuel pump off a Pontiac without running it up on the rack. I didn't have the right wrench anyway. I was going to have to beef with the kid that was on nights one of these days. He was supposed to pump gas and generally work around, but he was pretty absent-minded about tools besides.

I could say something to Carroll about it but I couldn't prove anything. It was his idea I had to leave my box open. Anyhow, if I blew him off he would send the work to the Shell across the street, like before, and just pick up his percentage for nothing,

When I wasn't working, in the past, it seemed as if there were plenty of jobs all over town. You know how that goes, when you're not looking for something. But now there wasn't any kind of profit in hustling anything, and I'd had to brace Carroll awhile for this job even, because of that County jerk time. There wasn't anything else. It's pretty quiet for everything today, it seems like, and still nobody is starving. That's the way it is, though.

I heard this horn tap, then, twice. I looked up. Madrid's Plymouth was out there on the blacktop. He was early. He was stopped by the recaps Big Willy had set out around the flag mast. I wiped my hands and went into the stockroom and took my wallet out of my slacks.

I was counting it as I came toward his car. For a moment I thought there was someone with him. It was one of those breezy sunny mornings, and all the little colored pennants that are wired to the office roof, stringing out to the pumps overhang and the flagpole, were looking perky and bright. I thought Lona just might be with him but, of course, she wasn't. He was alone. I didn't know what had made me think she would be.

"Well, there it is," I said to him. I handed him the seventy dollars through the window.

"Did you take your end out?"

"What do you think?"

"Take fifteen. How's that?"

I put the bills in my pocket.

He grinned. "You rub too easy, man. You don't want to jump so quick. Hell, look at me. I haven't been p.o.'d since last Tuesday."

He looked it. His eyes were like hard-boiled eggs with the white crut in the inside corners. But that could have been tiredness also. He had on his tan uniform shirt and the trousers. He must have come right off work, I thought, then driven almost two hundred miles to get here. Just to pick up fifty-five dollars that was his to start with.

He leaned over and opened the glove compartment. He reached under some blue paper windshield towels, and I could see his gun and cartridge belt rolled up inside there. He pulled out a bottle of vodka from underneath them. That was why I hadn't smelled a breath on him. That stuff doesn't leave anything on you.

"Get in, be sociable, hombre. Have a couple of snorts."

I looked over at the pumps. Big Willy was alone in front. The other two grease monkeys were over at the Rexall having coffee. That was Big Willy's business.

I got in the Plymouth and he handed me the bottle.

We went out the old Pike. When we hit the stretch where they've started to asphalt over the car tracks I saw trolley buses were using the overhead wires. I took a drink. It was hot and I felt sweaty and greasy. Only a handful of cars were on the road. I don't know where they go at eleven in the morning, but they weren't around there.

We had a couple of swigs apiece. "We need something to chase this lush," he said then. He stopped outside a Jap market. I watched him go inside, walking with a sort of roll, not actually squat but heavy, blocky, moving like some brown bear.

Then it hit me, all of a sudden. I could feel it down, pretty cold, inside me. I had been all right for two years, at least after a while. And now, I knew, it wasn't any use. And it wasn't the drinking now that was bringing it back. That had never done anything anyway.

Well, we'd had it, that first thing, in my V-8. Lona and I. All right, that's just a christening. But that's the way it happened, and I had never forgotten it really. Maybe because you remember the silly things the best. Well, we had plenty of that, then. And now I couldn't stand to think of any of it. I could even feel, sense her in his car now. It was that way. Like I had had the dumb thought she might be along when he drove up to Carroll's.

I watched him come back to the car. I wondered what my friends would say, they probably wouldn't speak to me for a month, going riding and drinking with a heat. With him, especially.

I handed him the fifth after he started up. He had a Squirt open, then passed both bottles to me. I took a good one and chased it. I sat back, feeling pretty double-barreled then. I was thinking, I can leave him alone right now; I can put him down, and whatever he has to say to me, because there's something. Before he got around to asking me out to a home-cooked dinner.

He was pretty likely to do that.

He slowed down, by one of the furnished apartment units that seem to be going up everywhere you look. Wherever they find the parties with the money for those places. They probably make it in the summer, when the beach gets the tourist play and all.

There was a sign, PROSPECTS PARK HERE. The units weren't finished though, and I couldn't see anyone around.

He parked in the driveway leading to the carports in back. Then he left the radio on; like it was just where I had come in the last time.

"I got a couple more things for you to hustle, Nick."

I took a swig. A little ran down my chin.

"You must be in some business," I said.

"You interested?"

"I'll drink anybody's booze and listen to them."

"Sure, go ahead. This home movie camera, and the projector goes with it."

"Got a cigarette?"

"Up there."

I felt along the sun visor and found the pack.

"What did you need those for?" I asked him.

"Lona wanted the stuff." He shrugged. "So I went for it. You get sold a bum deal, you know? They cost three-fifty-some damn bucks altogether. Now I got to peddle them."

"Where did all these bills come from? What kind of bills did you say you had?"

"Don't sound me, man. Just all of a sudden, you

know? A pile-up from things. You get a lot of stuff, use it a little, then put it away some place. Everybody's got one of those closets."

"But they still have to make the payments."

"That don't concern me."

"Nor me either. Not if the stuff wasn't mine."

"Don't worry yourself then. Hey, what did you say?"

"I wouldn't worry."

"Hell, who you think you're doing business with, anyway?"

"I don't know what I'm doing with you."

"Well, this's is no monkey business, see?"

"Well, what have you been doing?" I said. "You've been living pretty high, haven't you? Tape recorders, movie cameras—"

"You don't want the deal?"

"You haven't mentioned what it is, have you? Give me some of that."

He passed me the bottle.

"You ask two hundred, it's dirt cheap. Because the stuff is like brand new. And you get thirty-five."

I thought for a minute.

"Not by tomorrow. It'll have to be the day after."

"You want to look at the goodies? In the trunk."

"No." I looked out the windshield. "You wouldn't know where I live, by any chance?" I looked at him.

"Sure. In the phone book. I went by there the other day when I was looking for you."

"I'll have to put an alias in next time."

"Put one I wouldn't know, man." He grinned.

"You catch on. You can leave the things up there. The door's open."

"Can you lock it?"

"If you want to."

"You never know who's thieving around."

"I guess you would know better about that."

"You want another drink?"

"Aren't you afraid to drink in a car?"

"No. Are you?"

"No. But I've got to get back there."

"Have one anyhow."

So I did.

"You looked real funny working there, man, Hell, a hustler like you, in a gas station."

"Crut," I said. "And what was it you're supposed to be?"

As we came into the station, Carroll was backing his car against the fence. He got out and put his FOR SALE sign on the windshield. But that iron couldn't go down a hill in high. Then Madrid drove off and I went back to fooling with the Pontiac.

I watched Carroll go toward the office, in his green suit and green hat with the feather. He was coming from a Lions Club or a Chamber of Commerce brunch. His wife wouldn't let him out at night because she didn't trust him, so he got loaded a couple of times a week at daytime businessmen's affairs. I don't know what he was trying to prove that way. But that Carroll was nothing but a big farmer at heart. Bigger than Big Willy, even.

I bent over the Pontiac's fender. Then I felt this dizziness come over me suddenly. I shut my eyes for a second, waiting for it to pass. But it didn't. Then I didn't dare swallow.

I got my head out from under the hood and started walking, with the whole thing there in my throat halfway to the washroom. I was lucky to make it, all right. But I hadn't had it like that in a long time. I couldn't understand it coming on from that little drinking.

I washed my face and came out, the light hitting my eyes like some flicked rag.

I went into the office and Carroll was there behind the desk. He looked pretty wiped himself. He had that silly green hat on, going over the night kid's tickets with Big Willy.

I told him I would have to knock off. He said later on it, and I told him the hell with that, with that hat making me sicker, even. He asked me if I'd been drinking, and I asked him did he think he could tell. I asked Big Willy if he would look at the Pontiac, and he said something. I walked out of there, then, with the two of them looking at each other.

I got into my street clothes; then I went over and locked my tool box, skidding it under the bench. I got my Ford out from by the fence. I popped the clutch, accidentally spraying gravel over the colored kid Leroy that washes cars. He yelled something, but I bugged out into the street.

Down the line I pulled over and went into Saxie's. Saxie fixed me a bromo that almost took off my ears. Then, after a few minutes, I ordered a whisky sour. I sat there, smoking a cigarette, watching Saxie and his wife take the back-bar inventory. I felt like a woman drinking from that fancy little glass. But the sour stayed down, and I had another, and I was a lot better off then. And I knew what the trouble was, too. Because any drinking will put you down twice as fast when you're running too many things through your head all at once.

I felt good enough to go home, then. Instead, I split for the beach.

The old V-8 was running smoothly, purring. I had worked on her half of the Sunday before. There's no car with more when they're right; nor worse when they aren't. Sometimes, coming off a bum kick, I would get in her and fire hell out of her. She would be all I had then. She was old and stick-shifted, but there were these things I'd done to her. And she would run like this now, and I would get some of it off her, get to feeling that good then that I could stomp anything.

I reached my trunks off the window shelf, changing in her up on the highway. I went down across the beach and into the water. I went out quite a way before I began to feel it. I was almost out to where there's the troll fishing. Then I trod water. Out there the whole thing looked like some picture.

Some big pretty picture. The big, dynamited cliffs that were still sliding down blocking the highway, and the tourist motels on the edge, all glass, white-and blue-painted, the big palms up along the causeway, the gold-roofed Bay Club down the coastline a way, and even Buddy's Rancho back in the hills, that I had never seen before, like I had never seen any of it before.

I came back in, found a quiet spot, and lay down. I put my towel over my eyes. There was the light breeze that's sometimes close to the sand but doesn't stir it.

Those beach bums had nothing on me, I was thinking. Except I couldn't put one thing out of my mind. I had a feeling something was going to happen; maybe something was going to break for me finally. Now, after two years. I could almost feel it.

Because there is nothing really harder to find than a cop who's become a thief.

And one had come two hundred miles, looking for me.

THREE

I held my hand out the window, feeling the speed-wind burn my palm. I was doing eighty, but the block gauge was standing at F. I knew she wouldn't blow running, but I stepped her up anyway. Going off there a little, now slowly moving away, the hills were turning blacker in their own shade.

I brought up plenty of highway mirages. Not this big earthmover now, though, standing up big as hell. A sombreroed colored guy was driving, half asleep, in the bucket seat. I could raise him with my beer can, I thought. Except I wasn't done with it yet.

I heard the siren, then. It was the highway heat, their red lights coming up fast in the mirror. Those black and white birds weren't after me, though. They weren't supposed to bother you out here much under ninety. But you never looked over at them anyway.

I felt her wind-rock as they passed. That highway patrol Olds was moving, all right. I threw my beer empty after it.

I had a six-pack of Lucky on the floorboard, and a pack of empties on the back seat. I had been swinging since yesterday, last night. I hadn't been to bed yet. Well, later on it. Hell, later, later.

My radio was still out though, and I missed it. I'd pulled the chassis a week ago, and there was fifteen dollars due on it, when I had it. But, hell, I had this crossbar lug wrench in the trunk that would ring like chimes against the jack on bumps.

I figured to make Madrid's town, Cuesta, pretty soon, from my map. The mesquite and cactus had run out a while back, and now the mountains were widening up. Now there was nothing but the bare reaches of plains going up to the lava-rock hills. But I was glad I wouldn't have to cross those desert sandhills, all right.

Up ahead, the police Olds was passing some cars, making plenty of oil smoke. An ambulance went by, its siren and air horn going. You knew something had happened up there. Maybe someone was driving when they should have stayed drinking.

Then, as I came over the road rise, there it was.

It was a bad one. The way it looked, it seemed like the Studebaker coupe had hit the Buick sedan that was smashed to hell in front, then, coming off, had sideswiped this Ford convertible. The Ford was turned over on the shoulder and the Studie had rolled a couple of times too. That was how the thing looked all right: the Studie trying to pass, when the old Buick caught it coming on, caroming it into the Ford.

The cops kept the cars moving, but I saw these three bodies under sheets. One, with levi-topped boots sticking out, was lying by the old Buick, that was gyp-painted purple, and had a Mexico plate on the back. One of the white coats from the ambulance was working on someone in the back of the Buick. There was plenty of water and oil slicked over the highway, the combination smelling like machine coolant, stinking.

I was glad to let her out again, the tires oil-singing for a way. In the mirror all that splintered glass was reflecting, glittering like shaled ice in the sunlight.

I opened another can of beer. But the stuff wasn't cool anymore.

In a little while, the highway swung south, running

parallel to where the desert would begin. A double-decker Greyhound stood toward me, big as a locomotive, barreling. I stomped the accelerator, timing it to the gully bridge ahead.

The Greyhound seemed to lean toward me passing. Those gully-overs don't leave you much room for doubt.

I saw this lone filling station coming up then. I swung into it, stopping away from the pumps. I left her running, propping the beer carton across the accelerator. She would cool a little, idling fast.

The attendant sitting on the coke cooler didn't bat an eye at me. I went around to the back, then past some junked jalopies, through plenty of stinking broomweed. Then I had to come clear back and get the son of a bitch off the coke box for the key.

It was like a sweat box inside. I had to turn the water on under the tank. Outside the crickets were singing in the broom-grass. I flushed a water beetle down the sink drain. But it bubbled up and swam around. I looked around for a mirror, but there wouldn't be one.

I knew I needed a shave, all right; and a haircut too, sometime. I took my comb out, using it by feel. Then I dropped the key, that was wired to a piece of aluminum, into the raunchy toilet. It was a crummy thing to do. But I was pretty sore at that dead-butt grease monkey.

When he sounded me, I told him where I'd left his key. He got off the coke box, then. I saw him trying to get my number through the dust I put up in the mirror.

I thought about getting a shave when I hit the town, before I saw Lona. But then I thought the hell with it. And maybe with her, too. But we had had our times, all right. Balls, kiss-ups, some times.

But I was feeling pretty good, now, that I could put anything down. I'd had to drink nine cans to make it, that was good Lucky beer, too. But I finally had myself an edge. I took my jacket and shirt off, and was driving in my T-shirt. I could smell the tobacco from my cigarette. You only get things that clear at certain times. Like when someone lights up by you at the ballpark, or the peanut smell. But not at the night games, it's funny, or the fights. One thing was pretty much the same, though. Night or day. The hell you could say. I guess we'd made that almost every any way.

Well, you know the brass tubing that connects the bedposts across the top of an old flop? The time in this crummy pad: Lona, I'd tied her to that. Later, I went out for a drink, then untied her coming back. She couldn't stand for a while. Sure, it was a freak thing to do. But me sitting over there in that bar, thinking about her, and her back there, like that, still, thinking about me. Christ, all that unfinished business with us.

She was on horse, then. All right, yourself, too. Who isn't hooked on something? Just this little, anyway, with her. Because not the big scene, the main line, only skin pops. But thinking she was chippying on somebody was so funny, and pretty cute. Hell, you could be blind. Her always catching cold; running-nosed, itchy colds. But telling me no, then coming in, and straight, forgetting, asking me to please come turn on. But I had never gone that route.

But she got off the stuff. If you didn't goof heavily, you could make yourself come off it. But those needle scratches didn't go. The heat busted you just for marks these days, too. But not a cop's wife. Nobody would touch her. Only that Madrid. But never the way I had.

I was feeling good enough now, the way when you want to do something silly. Like throw her in second at seventy. And dig some hole in the road.

There was this roadside liquor store ahead. I let her drop off a little. Then, around fifty, I double-clutched her, turning off to come in. There was this gravel parking in front, and as I let up the clutch her back end swung, swinging, buckshotting the gravel; then when she began coming around I spun the wheel in that stuff, bringing her up broadside to the store entrance, not killing the engine, just touching the brakes.

An old boy came out, banging the screen door against the fender. I got out and grinned at him. He was skinny, red-faced as a turkey gobbler. I didn't listen to his spouting. I went inside. I bought a pint of bourbon from him. It was too hot anymore to keep beer in the car.

I took out my wallet, then I saw him looking at my waist. When I had taken off my jacket I had forgotten the .38 I was wearing inside my belt.

I paid him and got out of there.

Well, I wouldn't take a chance with that Madrid, you know. Not one if he did happen to see me with her. I really didn't know how stupid he might try to get. And I didn't know where he might be. So that was why the piece. But I didn't know why, exactly, because I couldn't see how I would use it. Anyway, I'd borrowed it from Sand-o, my old partner-in-crime. I thought it was an idea. The two of us had never stomped into any places together. Nothing in that line. I didn't know if Sand-o ever had alone, I doubted that.

Collecting guns was Sand-o's hobby. If things ever got that bad someday we figured we could go in a place like the Chinese army.

We would go up around Lancaster sometimes, in back of those long ranges of hills. Sand-o would have his M-1, and I'd have Sand-o's Winchester. We would blast plenty of beer cans, with Graemie boy sitting on a rock, high using grass, throwing a fit off the action.

But that was before I took this gig with Carroll. Because that was after someone turned rat in the crowd, and practically all the connections were busted. The way that happened, you see, the heat picked me up first, and kept me for seventy-one and a half hours, without booking me. That was all they did, but it was enough. Because the bad thing was some of the crowd thought I'd copped out. But, hell, I wasn't allowed even to make that one call out the law gives you. So nobody knew I was inside. And the heat working off my little black book you know, all those numbers, for three days. When I got out, I was a little while squaring myself around. But that had been quite a while ago.

And maybe now I didn't have a job, anymore, with Carroll. Who knew? I wasn't worried.

This way, going away from the desert now, the foothills were rolling, brush-covered. In the distance you could see the mountains hazed up behind them. Then I was in the Valley, and passing the big Association ranches, with the barracks on the edges for the Mexican pickers. Then a sign-board said you were about to enter Cuesta—to slow down. And it was just another of those melon- and cotton-picking towns.

I came past a ballfield, a couple of picnic areas, the

ice house, power plant, some farm-machinery-repair Quonsets, a few motels on the outskirts, gas stations with a war going down the main drag, a block with churches on both sides; then I hit the stores, and two- and three-story business buildings, and the square, with a statue of a cavalry officer in the middle, leading a charge.

I file-parked in the square and went into a drugstore. There was only one Madrid in the skinny phone book. I copied down the number and address. The girl behind the soda fountain told me where it was.

It was a small, cheap tract on the east edge of town. All the houses were box-like stucco jobs, and painted mostly the same shade of green. Some kids were playing around a milk truck on the street. I went by them slowly, checking the numbers. Then I made the house.

The old Plymouth wasn't in the carport. That didn't prove she didn't have it, and he was home. But if he answered, I would hang up and try later.

I stopped outside a gas station at the end of the block. I went into the outside phone booth. While the number was ringing, I looked over at the grease rack. An old blue coupe was on it, up in the air. I looked at it, closely. And then there wasn't any doubt about it. It was Madrid's Plymouth, all right.

"Hello?"

I couldn't see into the office. But if he was in there, he wouldn't have missed me through the front windows. "Hello? Hello?"

"Is Dave Madrid there?" I asked.

"Yes. But he's asleep just now. Who's this?"

Then I had to fish for a cigarette, all right.

"Nick, Lona. Nick Beniades."

There was a pause. Then, "Nick! Well, how about that. Where are you?"

"At the Chevron station, on your street."

"Out *here?* Well, why, Nick?"

"I want to talk to you about something. It's pretty important, Lona. Can you cut out for a while?"

"Oh? But I don't have the car, Nick. Dave left it when he got off work."

I looked over at the Plymouth, still nervous from what I'd thought. "Can I pick you up outside your house?"

"No, I don't think so, Nick. Let me think a minute—"

"Will he stay asleep?"

"Just like a baby."

"He's some baby."

"Now you come on. I know, Nick: when you hang up, turn right at the corner, then drive two blocks, and make a short right. You'll see a bunch of stores, with a parking lot in back. Park in there, and I'll walk over. What kind of car are you driving?"

"The old rod, still."

"Well, repainted, then?"

I was always getting her repainted; three times. "No, not since the last time. Maroon, still."

"You're in a rut, Nicky." She laughed. "Sure be real swell to see you, though. Can't you tell me what it's about, a little?"

"It'll wait. If you get a move on."

"I will. Same old Nicky, in a hurry. I'll hang up now. You're a mystery man, you know?"

"Sure," I told her.

I got into my car at the curb. I lit another cigarette. You could feel the heat now not driving. I wished I had my radio back.

FOUR

After a few minutes, the station's two grease monkeys came over to the pumps. One of them leaned on the cash box and the other stood by him. They were looking down the block. But I had already picked her up in the mirror.

It was a quiet street. Just those kids playing around the milk truck, and nothing else. Then she was in the blind spot, but there still in the side mirror. She had seen the car.

She was wearing a light green sweater, tucked into a pair of those bullfighter pants they've been wearing for a while. They were black and really tight. She'd had her hair dyed black, I saw, wearing it in bangs. It looked good. But it was still short, and close-curled in back, the way I'd always liked it.

The grease monkey leaning on the cash box straightened and spoke to her. The other one spoke to her then. They turned, then, watching her turn the corner. I started the motor.

I came up along the curb. She didn't look over, still. I got sore. I cut the ignition off then on, quick, then hit the gas. You know the noise baffled exhaust stacks can make?

I had to do it twice, though. Then she came over.

"Do you realize how many people are watching this?" She slammed the door getting in.

"Who was watching those grease monkeys?"

"What's wrong with their speaking to me?"

"You know me longer. And you haven't said go to hell, even."

"All right. There. Was there anything else you wanted?"

"Not right now, this minute."

"You're a doll. Will you please drive away from here now? I have friends around here, don't you think?"

"You have a friend here, too." I let in the clutch.

"Oh, is that what you are?"

"A real good friend."

"I saw something else, I thought."

I looked at her. "That's pretty good," I said. "For a short memory."

She looked out the window.

After a minute, though, she leaned over and took the cigarette from my mouth. Then I came into this undeveloped street: just these empty lots, run over with weeds. I could see the end of the main drag a few blocks over.

"Why are you stopping here?"

I took the butt from her and dragged on it. I reached past her and flipped it out the window.

"You almost had the filter," she said. "Nicky."

When I let her go, she was crying a little. I had felt her crying, I thought.

"Damn you, Nicky. Give me a cigarette. Oh, damn, damn you."

"What's the matter?"

"You shouldn't have done that."

I kissed her again. Then she pushed away from me.

"Oh, it's a wrong thing to say. But he's never kissed me like that."

"He didn't have smoke in his mouth."

"You didn't."

"I'll give him a couple of lessons sometime, if you'd like."

"You'd look real funny."

"I'll bet you look pretty funny with him."

"You stop that. Oh, let's get away from here. Give me a cigarette. No, hold my hand, it's shaking. Oh, Nicky, what are you doing out here?"

I shifted, driving one-handed. "How does that go?" I asked her. "You know, what they say about married life?"

"Why did you have to say that?" She pulled away. "Don't bring me, Nicky. You haven't changed. You were always so one-way. One kiss." She shook her head. "It's ridiculous."

"Sure."

"Nicky." Then I felt her hand again. "I'm the biggest liar."

Then I was past the town, back up on the highway, going south. I made the telephone poles go like fence pickets.

I saw this dirt road, all of a sudden, this cut-off. I had to take it hard, the front shocks banging. I scratched the whole one side against some mesquite bushes. I felt the crankcase underscraping hard too. I bumped along a way, the brush getting thicker alongside.

There were these few skinny cottonwoods ahead, the road going around the clump of them, on both sides. I figured there was a house somewhere at the end. I backed up around the trees, then, facing the way we had come.

I couldn't see the highway. Just the brush and plenty of dust rising.

I cut the ignition. Then I took her and kissed her.

"We're still good for each other, Nicky," she said. "We always were, weren't we?"

"You just forgot."

"How could I forget?"

"You did."

"Don't rub that in, Nicky. Not that now. I always needed somebody; someone. You know the way I am. That's the way I am. I can't help it."

"I didn't need anybody."

"Not in the County. You were inside, that was different."

"I guess it was."

"You're different, Nicky. Not like me—that way. Oh, don't hassle with me now, please. Don't get bitter on me."

"I'm not bitter. Don't kid yourself," I said.

"Just the way you say it. Well, it's no use."

I took her arm. "He moved himself in." She turned away and I swung her back. "In my pad. Tell me about that scene."

In the light her eyes would change, become this lighter,   hazel color. They were deep-set, and she used that brush stuff on the lashes that's supposed to make them seem sort of secret. But they always were that way to me. The stuff had run a little.

Then I couldn't look at her. I never really, actually could, it's funny. Except when I was drinking, or would be high. Then it wouldn't be there so much, what she had for me. Because I couldn't feel it.

"Forget it," I told her. "I'm sorry."

She didn't come on to me, though; didn't kiss me back. I opened my eyes and she was looking at me. She sat there, her head back on the seat, not saying anything. I had unbuttoned her sweater partly and I felt like a damn fool. It was quiet, and I could hear the cars going by on the highway.

I took the pint from the glove compartment. I cut the cap off with the ignition key. Then I got out of the car.

I went through the brush. There was this clearing, yellow-grassed, where the ground rose, and I could see the highway then plainly. I had a drink and put the cap on.

She was almost next to me before I heard her. She must have found a way through the brush. She looked up at me. I thought about how I would put a hand on her shoulder sometimes walking. I looked over at the highway. There was a lot of brush in between there all right.

"Are you going to offer me one?"

I unscrewed the cap and gave her the pint.

She made a face taking one. She hadn't changed, except for the darker hair now. It went with her being half Italian, but it made her look pale in that light. She was always pale, though, pretty white-looking; that went with her too. It was true, even, she looked her best when she wasn't feeling well. Then her cheekbones would stand out, her eyes look at you, pretty deep, pretty secret.

"I wanted to visit you, Nicky. But he told me not to go downtown. He didn't want it known that I knew you."

"Leave it alone," I said.

"You know, I'd clue you on something. But you wouldn't understand."

"There's that chance."

"He asked me to marry him."

"Did you have him tell me that?"

"What do you mean?"

"Skip it."

"I knew you wouldn't understand."

"Oh, Christ, Lona," I said. "A heat. A narco heat."

"He wasn't the kind of cop you think. He lost his job because of me."

"He kept you from going to jail. Did that help you decide about marrying him?"

"He was good to me. Real good."

"For a heat."

"Or anyone else."

"You should know," I said. But I didn't mean it.

"I don't care what you say."

"Crut," I said.

"That's all you can say."

I took the bottle from her. The stuff went down wrong and I coughed. I spit. I looked at her. "He's something else, besides playing the law. He's a thief. Maybe you know about that?"

"What are you talking about?"

"I've been working with him. That's all. Fencing these things he's been thieving."

"You're a liar. What things?"

"A tape recorder, and some home movie equipment. He scammed me the stuff was yours."

"He's crazy. You're crazy. You're a liar."

"All right. How much do you want?"

"Don't scam me, Nicky."

"I never did, did I?"

"You've beaten me for so many things."

"There you go. Listen, have I ever lied to you?"

"No, that's true. Give me a drink."

She took one.

"What's there to cry about?" I asked her.

She turned her head.

"Not because he's a thief?"

She shook my hand off and stepped back. She had on those ballet kind of slippers and one came off. She tried to put it on one-handed, holding the pint, and sat down on the grass. You couldn't laugh at her. Then she threw the slipper away from her.

"Why can't things ever work out? Why can't they?"

I knelt by her. "Have another drink," I told her.

"Don't order me. I always hated that in you."

"I asked you."

"You never asked anything. You took, and you beat. You know that's true."

"I just remembered something. Lush and you never mixed."

She had one then. "Well, neither did you and me. You hurt me in a whole bunch of ways. Little ways. You don't know how badly."

"Tell me," I said.

"You wouldn't work. That was one. Nicky take a gig? No, Nicky was a character. Nicky was a hustler. Gigs were for squares."

"When did it change?"

"When your friends went to work. And they were characters. But when there wasn't any hustling, they went to work. But you didn't. You sponged off your friends, and beat them for money."

"They were my friends."

"They were mine too."

"I should have asked you first."

"I wanted to be proud of you. And I was, sometimes, so proud. When you wanted to, you could be so wonderful. You don't know how cool you could be."

"Why bring it up now?"

"Do you remember when I was turning tricks?"

"I told you to do that, didn't I?"

"Don't be so snotty. But you knew it, and ate off me. And I paid the rent more times than I didn't. Who paid it when you were in the County?"

"You had a better chance to."

"So it was my pad, then, not yours. And he *didn't* move in on you."

"That's a nice technical point. Listen, lay off that. You're lushed enough."

"So I wanted to get away from all characters, and damn character-isms. So I wouldn't be hurt anymore. I didn't want to swing anymore. You wouldn't believe that, but it's true. And I tried to make him a good wife. I tried—don't laugh. Then, when we would make it I would see it in him, looking at me. Him thinking about the way I was coming on, and the others I'd been with, because I'd told him everything. And I knew things weren't going to change, just because I wanted to. Because you can't change what's happened. You can't."

She was crying.

I took the pint from her and had one. "Flush him," I said.

"No. I'm no good, Nicky. I'm no good for anybody. It's me."

"That's a scam."

"He wasn't a thief when I married him. Or anything else."

"Well, you didn't turn him out. Where's the money going, anyhow, do you think?"

She closed her eyes. Then she shook her head to herself. "I don't want to think about it. Maybe he's chippying on me, do you think? That would be all right, I wouldn't much blame him. I've been awfully snotty to him besides. I used to be after him to get off the graveyard shift. I didn't like being alone nights."

"He likes it good. Because that must be when he heists the stuff. Have there been any store burglaries around here?"

"Oh, I don't know. I don't know."

"I figure he's working by himself. While he's on duty. It's a setup. There isn't much money in it, that's why I think he's pulled it more than once. But I can't figure what's turned him."

"He's not satisfied with his job. That's the truth. He can't get ahead because of the politics they play, he says."

"That might be it. It could fit."

"You mean you think he's getting even with the department?"

"It depends how he thinks. He's got some reason besides the money. When you're sore enough you'll do some screwball things."

She was looking at me, smiling a little. She rubbed her nose. It was pretty perfect, thin-boned and hardly tilted. "I'm sorry, Nicky. I didn't mean to come on that way, either."

"You were mostly right."

"You come here now. Come here."

I came closer and knelt by her. She put her arms around my neck. "Are you going with any girls, Nicky?"

"No. Nothing's been happening."

"You must be really hard up." She grinned.

"Nothing in particular."

"Sometimes I'd think, maybe Nicky has himself a square chick now. Wouldn't that be a gas?"

"Something."

"I wish I had the old Nicky again. That's what I'd like. I wish things were back the old way again."

"I wouldn't have thought so."

"You should have put your hand across my mouth. You know me."

"That's right."

"Remember how you used to take care of me, Nicky? When I'd be unreasonable sometimes?"

"Yes."

She pulled out a blade of grass, studying it.

"That always sort of worked, didn't it?"

"Yes," I said.

"*Yes.* Oh, Nicky. What's the matter?"

"Nothing's the matter."

She looked around, over her shoulder, at the brush beyond. "Well, is there *anything* in the car?"

"In the trunk. The G. I."

"If I remember you. It scratches your back. Oh, Nicky. What's the *matter* with you?"

"What about him?"

"I don't care about him, now."

"Anymore?"

"Maybe I never really did. I don't know. Do you see what you make me say?"

"Anymore," I told her. I looked at her.

"Yes. Oh, yes. Anymore."

FIVE

When I drove into Carroll's, the kid on nights was hosing down the blacktop. I was a few minutes early, but he was late going off. Big Willy was switching the tires on a Buick alongside my bench. The other two front men hadn't come in yet.

I parked and Big Willy looked up from beside the Buick as I walked in.

"The man said not to change into your whites, Nick."

"How's that?"

"He's pretty hot on you not calling in yesterday."

That was Big Willy. He had heard Carroll say he was going to bag me probably. But he's one of those people who can't come right out with anything. He squinted up at me as I came over.

"Well, he knows what he can do about it. Anytime."

"That's what it sounds like. I think. He said you're to come back at noon."

Well, there it was. I had the old can tied to me. Carroll was quick.

"Has he got anyone to replace me?"

"He doesn't want any more temperamental mechanics, he says. I think he meant this Jess, more likely, that was here before you. He's thinking of sending the jobs across the street again."

"That's a good idea for him."

"They get a lot of comeback on their work, though."

"Well," I told Big Willy. "That's that, I guess. Can I show you anything around?"

"I looked around some. Oh, did you see the cotter keys? I packed the bearings on this crate. I found a couple in your drawer."

I told him where the can was. Then I got my box and things and put them in my Ford. I got a battery I had in the stockroom and put it behind the seat.

I stopped by the cooler for an orange soda as the two pump men drove in. They were a couple of slouch-shouldered, sideburned kids who roomed together. I thought they were knocking down on Carroll. If they weren't I was pretty wrong about them.

Then I went over to Big Willy down beside the Buick. "Well," I told him, "have fun."

"What you figuring on doing?"

"I won't kick any horse apples down the street. Don't worry."

"You want me to drop your dough by your room later? Carroll was figuring what you had coming."

"Hell, if you feel like it. Fine. I'll have a beer for you." I could get along all right without seeing Carroll any more.

"I'll come by on my lunch time. You be in around twelve?"

"If I'm not, look in the refrigerator." Big Willy had stopped by my pad a couple of times after work. Big Willy was fat, bald, and pretty square. He'd asked me if I couldn't fix him up with a woman. Just to go out with. But I didn't know anyone that would be interested.

I put the orange bottle in the wire rack. As I was driving out, the colored washer, Leroy, came out and waved to me. He was trying to get on special with the post office, and I was rooting for him to make it.

I stopped by Louis'. Some graveyard workers with Douglas Aircraft badges and a few early winos were at the bar. Louis had been opening at six since The

Wheel across the street started opening early that summer. But Louis hadn't got any of that cycle-club trade.

I asked Garland, who'd opened, if Sand-o had left a message for me. I had stopped in when I got back to town the night before, but left early. Garland looked at the pad on the back-bar. My note to Sand-o was gone, was all. Garland brought me a cup of coffee, then I left.

I drove up Vista to Minoso. I made a U on Minoso, then I backed up into Omar Lane. Omar is a small dead-end, and this time Shirley gave one of her jive parties I had backed through the big shrubs in front of those El Contento Courts, trying to turn around. That cost me thirty dollars when I was eating at the Fresno Market lunch counter twice a day to get the coffee refills. So now I backed into the street.

Shirley's was one of those small one-room and kitchen bungalows with a one-half after the number. There's plenty of shrubbery around in the back that's handy for Shirley's outside grass stashes.

I gave Shirley's knock. I heard bare feet coming across the floor, then Sand-o opened the door. He was in the raw. I followed him through the kitchen, and Shirley was asleep inside in the hideaway bed. Sand-o got back in beside her and shook her. "Hombre's here."

She raised her head. "Hi, Nick."

"Hi, Shirl," I said.

I sat down in the only chair there was space for in the room. Sand-o had brought it from the shop where he worked when he moved in with Shirley. Sand-o upholstered bar stools and booths when there was a call for him. It was good hourly wages, but took plenty of strength in one hand and arm, pulling the covers over the padding for tacking. But Sand-o had it made there.

I waited while he rubbed his neck to come awake. Sand-o was blond and wore one of those Caesar crewcuts with the bangs-like in front, and had muscles like sacked potatoes, except in one arm. He had smashed up the left one in a car accident, breaking it in four places, and they'd had to re-break it twice to set it, and then it never came back normal. He called it his baby arm once, but then he was pretty lushed. It was only about half the size of the other one. But he made up for it with the right. He was my height, six feet, but one ninety-five to my one seventy.

Sand-o was on this perpetual health kick. When he had a candy-vending route going for him he had this outboard he would trailer out to the Salton Sea, or down to Mission Beach, for water-skiing weekends. Then things got slow so he had to peddle his machines and hang out at Muscle Beach again. He'd met Lona at the Beach, originally. He'd taught her to lift some of the weights there with him, before he hurt his arm. It was Sand-o who'd turned Lona on grass and showed her some other things first. But that weight-pressing turned her around inside, so she couldn't have kids. I'd known Lona to speak to in Compton College, then I started going around with her. I brought her over into the crowd. But Sand-o was her teacher.

"What's happening, hombre?" he asked me.

"Carroll got to me. I was fired."

"That what your note was about? You said maybe you had something, didn't you?"

"Maybe," I said, meaning, Shirley, who was waking up.

"I'm hip," he said.

I lit a cigarette while he went into the shower. He ran the water, then yelled for me to have a beer. I opened a can from the refrigerator and came back to the chair. Shirley's parakeet flew in from the kitchen and landed on my shoe. It pecked the tips off your laces but I left it there.

I picked up one of Shirley's Brubeck albums. The window shade was pulled down behind me and I turned on the floor cone lamp to read the piece on the lining. This spooky blue light came on. The last time I remembered, Shirley's sex light had been red.

She sat up in the pull-out, tucking the sheet under her arms. Shirley wasn't bad-looking. She was a dishwater blonde, with these cow eyes, but a sexy mouth.

"Give us a drag, hombre?" she said to me.

I gave her my cigarette. She dragged on it. "Now I'm loaded again. Lois and John were over last night. You know John, don't you, hombre?"

I didn't know John was out. He'd been in San Quentin a year or more for hit-and-run.

"The parole board saw things John's way. The joint's no good for John, hombre. He couldn't make it up at Q. He's too quiet, inside himself, you know? But John is real folks, hombre."

"There's plenty of good people up north, I guess."

"I know, but you know? Say, touch me. This is the first cigarette I've had today."

I grinned at her. She was still a little loaded. The place smelled of jive.

"Hombre, we turned on one. The four of us. Turned old me on, then turned me out. You should have been here, doll."

"I would have been the fifth."

"Cool. We wanted to get a chain scene going, but that Lois just wanted to watch. Then she came in. She acts so damn square sometimes I don't know what to tell you. You've met Neray, haven't you—the cute little Chinese chick? She was coming over alone. It's a gas the way she drives around all night *so-o* loaded in her funny old Cad."

"I'll listen about her."

"She didn't show. Later on you, doll; like tomorrow. I could have eyes along those lines, myself. Where were you, anyway?"

Shirley ran her mouth too much. She talked a streak when she was straight. "I went around," I told her. I'd come over to fan with Sand-o a little, figuring she would be up and gone to work.

She poked in the ashtray on the built-in shelf the hide-away stowed beneath. She picked out this cocktail, then brought out a roach holder from the back of her clock radio. Shirley kept the radio stores busy replacing the alligator clamps she took out and used for roach holders. She clipped the holder to the cocktail and touched her lighter to it. I bent over and took a drag, with her holding. I sat back in the chair and took a swig of beer. Shirley's cocktails were nothing more than the coal of the marijuana. They cut hell out of your throat.

Sand-o came out of the head with a towel around him. She held him up a toke. The sheet slipped a little on her, and she had nothing on, and I saw she was as big out as ever up here. I'd made out with Shirley a couple of times, before Sand-o started living with her.

"Don't come on crutty to Nick," Sand-o said to her.

She looked up at him standing beside the bed.

"Come on. Break out a joint, Jesus."

Shirley shrugged. The cocktail was gone. She reached inside the radio and took out a joint. It was a dumb stash all right; one of the first places the law always looked. I knew it wasn't Sand-o's stash.

"We had to drive to Long Beach to score last night, hombre. We used Shirley's Chevvy and gas. That's why Shirley's so chintzy."

"Cocktails are supposed to be the real pod," I said.

"That's your joint. I made it for you."

"We were lucky to score at all. But it's green grass," Shirley said.

Sand-o rolled a nice tight marijuana joint. They burned slowly and stayed lit. I licked the paper on the sides to slow the burning. I lit the joint, then passed it to Sand-o. He passed it to Shirley. She toked, then dragged on a fresh cigarette I'd given her. You can climb fast doing that.

Sand-o put on his manila cords and boots. He put on one of his specially made sport shirts, with one sleeve shorter, and buttoned the cuffs. He took some paper handkerchiefs from Shirley's stash shelf and blew his nose carefully. Sand-o had that nasal drip thing. He broke his nose when he was playing ball in school, which probably didn't help. His sister had a broken nose, too. But they were a big, good-looking family.

Shirley passed me the joint, and I passed to Sand-o. He had Shirley's parakeet on his finger. He dragged and holding the bird close, blew the smoke on it. The parakeet shook its head but didn't fly off. It was a swinging bird, Shirley said. Sand-o put it on his shoulder and went into the kitchen. The refrigerator shut, then there were beer can tops buckling. Sand-o came in with the three cans, and stopped.

"Listen. You hear anything?"

"That's thunder," I said. My own ears were ringing.

"I'm loaded," Shirley said. "Loaded-ed."

I didn't want to get straight. But it was too late now.

Sand-o sat on the floor with his beer, leaning against the unpainted record cabinet he'd made for Shirley. I moved the chair up so I could reach her on the bed and Sand-o now to pass to him. I passed myself one time. The roach was a cocktail now practically and Shirley had her holder on it. You could hear the hiss of air sucking as Sand-o took a deep drag, then holding the smoke, not talking, kept his head down to get the pod working. Then he passed the cocktail to Shirley to keep going.

"You got—any beef—with—Carroll?" he asked me, letting what smoke was left now come out.

"No. I just took the day off, and part of the one before. He hung the can to me for it."

"You didn't take anything else?"

"What else? I was glad to blow him off anyway."

"I'm hip. Don't put any clothes on," he said to Shirley. She'd put the cocktail in the ashtray and was getting out of bed. She just had pants on. She was a little thin, but big in the chest. Sand-o reached up and slapped her as she passed.

"I have to go to the gig today. Noon," he said to me. "This gin mill over in Hawthorne. It burned out last week. Fire in the head."

"Where in Hawthorne?" I asked him.

"There's a where there? Jesus. I don't know."

He got up, then, and sat on the bed while Shirley ran the shower.

I told him about Madrid. It was copping out, now,

because I'd said I was going out to the police range when he'd loaned me the .38. I told him what I'd been doing with Madrid, and then about my seeing Lona. I told him I was meeting Madrid today, but I didn't know if it was going to lead anywhere actually.

Sand-o knew Madrid by sight. Madrid used to drop into the Goodnight Bar. A lot of the sheriff's plainclothes heat, especially, went in there. Some of us would stop in after smoking jive, letting them smell it on our clothes for kicks. But wearing black glasses and cool, clean, nothing on us. That was before we learned to *be* cool, though. And that Goodnight wasn't the place.

I told Sand-o I would clue him if anything happened. That was all there was to say then. Sometimes it's true you can talk a thing out of happening. He put on a Shorty Rogers side and we had another beer, listening. I looked at the watercolor he'd tried his hand at for Shirley hanging there above the record player. It was a picture of a guy with a blond beard and wearing a king's crown. But the crown had turned out looking like one of those party favor hats.

I went into the head when Shirley came out. She had put on her makeup and a bathrobe. I looked at myself in the mirror. My eyes were that red, bloodshot all right. The comic books on the floor looked all jumbled up, and I could smell the Kress's incense, strong, that Shirley burned.

I came out and she was dressing to go to the barber shop where she worked. She always went in high, but using eye drops, and doing the customers' nails probably by memory. An ironing board leaning against the wall, with its legs folded across, looked like some big grasshopper ready to grab her. I giggled. I was loaded but I couldn't use it now. I had to be in my place for Madrid when he came by after checking at Carroll's.

I told Sand-o I had to cut out. He told me to finish my beer first. I started to lean on top of the television, then I felt something move under my shoe, flurrying, then go soft.

"Oh, Christ," I said, looking down.

Shirley pointed and screamed. She grabbed Sand-o's arm, screaming, and he pushed her onto the bed. He bent to the floor and then he was in the bathroom and the toilet flushing. He came out and shook Shirley to stop her.

"You mother—" she said to me, crying, and Sand-o slapped her. "You mothering Greek bastard," she yelled, fighting Sand-o, and he hit her in the stomach hard. She twisted on the bed, holding herself. She tried to grab the back of his shirt and he turned and hit her in the stomach again. Then she lay on her side, with the pillow over her face.

She was dressed ready to go to work, and I was sorry as all hell the thing had happened. She'd had that parakeet a long while, I knew. But it was always around your feet. Still, I felt pretty bad about it.

I told Sand-o I was sorry. I told him so long, then, and I went out.

SIX

I drove up to the Safeway, where I didn't know anyone, because I didn't have my dark glasses. I bought two quarts of milk, a jar of Skippy, and a box of crackers. I had pretty double vision when I came out, and it was too much like work to park in my space under my building. I parked in the street, came up to my room, then took a cold shower. I got dressed, then I slid the window open farther and set my card table next to it.

I ate the crackers and peanut butter, drinking the cold milk slowly. I watched the characters that hang around the Fresno Market lunch counter at the corner. I saw this Joey Webb that I hadn't seen in a long while. Then I began to stop swinging. But I wished I'd made that second quart chocolate. Then I heard a knock at the door. I said come in.

It was Madrid. He was dressed in a brown jacket, brown sports shirt, and slacks. He looked happy about something. I told him to sit on the bed while I finished.

"I looked at the station for you. They give you the air, eh, for taking time off?"

"No," I told him. "For free."

"That's a corny joke. It's too bad."

"No it isn't."

"You make another connection?"

"I've been sitting here waiting for you."

Joey Webb was doing a jig now in front of the Fresno. Joey was an ex-welterweight who'd had that one fight too many. I wondered where he'd been hanging out lately.

"You do all right for me, man? I don't want to rush you."

I put the milk in the refrigerator. Then I took the two hundred and twenty dollars out of my shoe in the closet.

"How much you get?"

"Count it."

Then he saw my red eyes. "Hell, you got a poke in the head, man? I thought I smelled that jive."

"How are you getting your kicks?" I asked him.

"You can put that stuff down, man."

"When I do, you'll be the first to know."

All he had asked for was the two hundred. But I hadn't held out the extra twenty, although I'd thought about it. Now I wished I had.

He gave me forty-five dollars though. Forty-five was all right, I figured.

I went over to the window. Someone had bought Joey Webb his coffee. He was drinking it and looking around him in that jerky way he had.

"You get what you needed to pay your bills?"

"This'll help. What you going to do for yours now?"

"I might park behind a store some night."

He laughed. "Don't park in alleys, man. That's bad."

"Why don't you tell me how to do it?"

"Stay away from the store alleys, man. That's for sure."

I turned around from the window. "Why don't you take some of your own advice?" I said. "Who have you been kidding?"

"Kidding who, hombre?"

"That's what I said. None of that junk I hustled belonged to you. Or anyone else. It wasn't used once, even."

"So? You think I lifted the stuff, eh? Where from?"

"Not the Salvation Army."

"You're pretty sharp, man."

"I know hot stuff when I see it."

"You do? Why'd you touch it then?"

"Just as a favor to you."

"*Cagada*," he said. That means crut in Spanish.

"You asked me the question."

"Why didn't you stop in to see me yesterday?" he said. "You were out my way, I think."

This piano teacher was practicing next door. With the loud pedal. She had a shower that dripped at night too.

And then it burned me, seeing him flopped on the bed there, thinking he really had me, smiling with those big white teeth. I thought, then, the hell with him. I didn't care if he knew I was out there, or what he might try.

"You're supposed to sleep sometime, aren't you?" I said to him.

"I'm a light sleeper, man. How come you came out?"

"I had the day off. I felt like taking a ride."

"That's a long drive."

"You haven't seemed to mind it."

"You picked up Lona, didn't you?"

"You're wasting your time, you know. You should buck to take the detective exams. Or have the politics got you stopped there, too?" I said to him.

"Oh? You know something funny, eh? What did Lona tell you, hombre?"

"Just that. That you were in line for sergeant once, but that this lieutenant has it in for you. He's prejudiced against Mexicans; especially if they're cops working for him."

His eyes lit a little. "You had your heads together, you and Lona. She tell you any other funny stories, man?"

"What other? Is that the way the ball curves out there? They pay you almost Mexican wages, don't they?"

"Don't let it bother you."

"I would be pretty sore if I were in your shoes, I guess. You were born in Arizona, weren't you? You were in the service too. What about your seniority?"

"I got enough to pull the graveyard shift—steady." Those teeth flashed. "Hombre—you try a little something with Lona, maybe?"

He was laying that pretty cold on me, I knew. Because he couldn't have gotten that out of Lona.

"You should have more confidence in yourself."

"Hell, man, you're the sucker." He laughed at that. "How did I figure you were in town? Not from Lona. She was asleep when I left this morning. Last night, when I come to work, they got a pickup on a red Ford: a lowered fifty-one coupe, possible L. A. serials. The guy driving is a dark-complexioned, has black hair, wears it long, has this split chin, and a straight nose. You're a good-looking guy, hombre. The guy had a T-shirt on and a gun in his belt. That liquor store man goofed your number, but I had a hunch on you from his description. You're lucky you didn't get picked up. What was the gun for, though? You bought that bottle. How many rabbits you miss coming out?"

"I thought I would get used to wearing a piece. I might run a job out your way some time. Or is there a law against that?"

"You don't want to be lushed on a job. That's for punks, hombre. Not you."

"You're the book of knowledge, aren't you?"

"I know how you don't pull a job, I can tell you."

"Why don't you try something good for yourself? With your experience. Or aren't you that bitter yet?"

"Maybe. Soon. I've been looking at a pretty big thing."

"Well, look at a bank for me, will you? While you're shopping. Any one will do."

"I've been looking at this bank, hombre."

"I'll bet you have."

"Four months, hombre."

"Looking all right. I'll buy that."

"That's right."

"O. K. I'll go along with a story. What are you going to do about it? Or wouldn't that be anyone's business?"

"Yours. If you're interested."

"Is that right?"

"Sure, hombre. That's right."

I could hardly hear the knock on the door with that piano playing going on. I went over and opened it. Big Willy was there. He handed me my pay envelope.

"I've got unexpected company," I told him. "Wait a second."

I shut the door halfway, then I took a can of beer from the refrigerator and opened it. I gave it to Big Willy. "Can you knock it off in your car?" I asked him.

"You bet, Nick. Well, be careful. Don't take any bum jobs."

"I'll watch it," I told him. "I'll see you around, Willy."

I shut the door, and Madrid looked up at me from the bed.

He had the pillow behind him and his feet up on the cover. I sat down in the chair and looked at him.

When he was through telling me this thing, he took

his shirt off and stretched out there on the bed.

I was supposed to go out and think his crazy idea over. That's what he had called it himself. I was supposed to get used to it before I decided. And I had to, all right. Because I didn't know, actually, what I'd been expecting of him. But it wasn't anything like this, now.

But when I came back, he said, he had to know how I stood. If I didn't go along with him, that was just the chance he had taken. But it wasn't one really. Because I wouldn't know where or when he had the thing set for. And if he went ahead without me, with one or two others he had in mind, he would be in Mexico if I talked, anyway. For all the good it would do me.

Then he was asleep, that quick, snoring face up. I went out and left him with that piano playing next door for accompaniment.

I walked up to the corner and stopped at the Fresno Market lunch counter for something. Joey Webb was still there, wearing his cap and somebody's sports jacket. I asked him where he was hanging out now, and he'd been in the County hospital with pneumonia. I gave him two nickels toward his bottle of wine. Joey just touched the people he knew, and then only light. He'd had some manager, you knew, to fix his face like that.

"*Gracias*, hombre," he told me, "my *amigo*." He had it in his head I was Mexican.

"*Segura*, Joey," I said.

I got my change from Mary and took my burger and coffee into one of the phone booths at the end of the counter. I called the shop where Sand-o worked, but he was already out on that Hawthorne job. I got the number and it rang a minute over there before someone answered. They called Sand-o in from outside.

Graemie was with him, Sand-o said. He'd got Graemie on for half a day because he was short, helping swamp the damaged booths and fixtures in the café onto the truck. They would be through around five. I told him I would pick him and Graemie up at the shop. Something had come up, I said, but I couldn't talk on the phone. Sand-o was a little sore I wouldn't clue him more. But I wanted to handle it that way.

I went back to the counter and got the free refill on my coffee from Mary. There's this box-like mirror deal set into the wall there above the counter. It's for the spotters to look down on the help. They can see out, but you can't tell when they're up there. It's probably necessary, but those spotters must cost more than any thieving they catch. I felt sorry for Mary having to work there. It's bad enough bringing time, punching a clock, without being watched by the hour.

I cashed Carroll's check at the liquor counter inside the market. I bought a half-quart can of beer, some razor blades, and a magazine. I thumbed through a couple of the art-picture magazines in the rack. Then I went outside, up past the lunch counter, and sat up in one of Eddie's chairs next to the phone booths.

Eddie gave me his opener and I poured him a beer in his coffee mug. I sat there while Eddie was giving me his wax shine, sipping beer and reading this magazine piece on Frank Sinatra.

I'd always envied Sinatra pretty much. I guess, mainly, because he said and did just about what he felt like. It was nothing to do with having money either, because he was the same way when he didn't have it there for a while. The time he couldn't get a job singing anymore, when nobody wanted him. He had this beef going all the time with newspapermen. But anything you do that the other guy figures he can't get away with, because he hasn't the guts to try it, he's going to say something about it.

I walked back to my car, then I decided to run over to the bank. The teller went over and read my card and I filled in the amount on my check for cash. He didn't ask me how I wanted it. Together with what I'd had in the bank, my paycheck money, and the forty-five from Madrid, I walked out of there with a hundred and sixty-three dollars. That was between me and the street. Any kid with a good paper route could have bought and sold me twice.

I drove around to the back of Doc's shack, and waited while my radio was being installed. It was good having it back again and I looked for some jazz on the band. But there wasn't any. I settled for some show tunes.

I still had plenty of time to kill so I got on the freeway and drove over to Hollywood. I drove down Sunset Boulevard to Western, then turned up into Griffith Park. The Observatory is up there, and you're supposed to see Catalina from that high when it isn't smoggy. But there was the stuff laying over Los Angeles, most of it settled downtown.

Two yellow school buses came up the hill, letting out a gang of yelling kids. Their teachers marched them into the Observatory, to catch the show on planets inside.

The last time I'd parked up at Griffith had been several years before. I had just got out of the Air Force, and had this date with Lona that night. We came to Hollywood for a drink, and then I drove up here. I'd been in basic training, and was unassigned at Santa

Ana, but I had enlisted on that cadet deal. Then I spent three days under observation and I was through the next week, washed out. I had this racing pulse, they found out, that was no good for flying. It hadn't shown up in the early physicals because I was taking something for them. But when I saw how things would be, I'd let it go that way. They would have washed me out sooner or later, I figured.

But I'd wanted to stay in. I was in the National Guard infantry in Korea, and wanted out then all right. But I wasn't doing anything for this long while, and then this cadet—flying—thing looked good. And I was just qualifying to knock it, you know, and then I was out.

That hit me pretty hard. I told Lona how I felt. Sitting in my Ford up in Griffith, with the lights of L. A. spread out there below, and Western Avenue this string of lights as far as you could see, but all that scenery was wasted on me. Because the way you go on when you're brought pretty badly. Because I had tried to get something going, and been talking it up pretty big, and now I was going to have to take that kidding. But Lona listened to me, wearing this white filmy dress that made her look less even than twenty-one at the time.

Then she told me. How she didn't know I wanted to get any place, but was just interested in having a time. And told me the way she felt, more than she probably should have, because she still hadn't known me for long. But I was to watch, things would change, wait and see. Because she felt that way about me.

And that was that first time between us. Because that was the way it happened, later, after a while. That was the way it was, but never really like that again. Plenty of times, after, but not exactly like that.

You never know how the time passes when you're sitting, just thinking. Because I heard those school buses starting up, then, and here were the kids coming out, yelling. I didn't wait for them to get on board. I wasn't going to smell those bus exhausts going down.

Before I pulled out, I took a look all around. It was a fine view, but you could take it for granted. Like you took anything, it seemed, if it was there all the time. Like I had been with Lona. And maybe she was with me, too.

And now I was supposed to think this thing over. Let him, Madrid, know just where I stood.

With Lona, all along, still, waiting for me.

SEVEN

Sand-o and Graemie were there on the corner. I blew my horn, double-parking in the traffic. It was still bright with the Daylight Saving and Graemie turned, blinking at the car.

I held the seat for him to get in back. Sand-o got in beside me and shut the door. The light changed and Graemie came forward against Sand-o's seat as I stopped.

"For Christ's sake," Sand-o told him.

"What's the latest, man?" Graemie asked me from the back. I hadn't seen him since Madrid came into Louis' looking for me.

"Graemie boy's up," Sand-o said. "I told him about you hustling those goodies for our friend, Officer Madrid."

"Well, he's graduated. He's got eyes for banks now."

The light turned green and I moved ahead in the traffic.

"What eyes? You mean *robbing* a bank?"

"That's what he says."

"Is he dingie?" Sand-o's mouth was nearly open.

"He's serious."

"You're kidding. Don't jive me."

"Not unless he is."

"Well, Christ Almighty. He's no damn bank robber."

"I guess he isn't. Neither are any of us."

"*Us?* What's that for?"

"He wants to stomp into a bank. There's no real money going inside one alone, with a gun in a paper sack. You just get the chicken feed from a teller's drawer. And if he doesn't give it to you you probably shoot him, then have to shoot your way out. It takes three to do it the right way. Two going inside, and the outside man. Then you're backed to sack up that vault loot."

Sand-o sucked his teeth. "And how much did you get from your last play?"

I hit him on the knee. "It doesn't count, Madrid says. The guys with experience have all been caught. If they're out, the heat looks for them after a big job. So he'd rather try it with greenhorns, like us."

"Oh, he would?"

"Because we've got not big-time records. I've been inside that once, you were up in Washington on that mastic-painting deal, and Graemie's been busted for grass and marks. But we never fell for that bank robbery."

"No, and I don't intend going to."

"He was just testing out that fencing on me. You know he could have handled it himself. So he thinks everything's pretty George now. He told me to sound you on this idea, especially. He remembers you around when he worked here. He says you seemed to be cool to him."

"Wasn't that around the time when he busted you?"

"All right, that was then. But now he's got this idea. I've just been listening to him, anyhow. I put Graemie up, and he'll see about him."

"He doesn't know about Graemie? Graemie boy's the coolest wig here. Look at him."

I could see Graemie in the mirror, sitting up straight back there in his shoulder-padded suit, his pop-eyes half closed, smiling to himself. He was straight all right. Not on grass either. "Your mother have any children?" he asked Sand-o.

"Your father didn't have you," Sand-o told him.

"Your mother," Graemie said.

"Well," Sand-o said to me, "I'm not pulling your sleeve, hombre. But a crooked fuzz can't come chilly enough for me. I wouldn't run with him into a five-and-ten, let alone some scam bank."

"Well, hell, I don't trust him, either."

"He's got your water on already for fencing that stuff. You're in his pocket."

"That can work two ways."

"You get a judge to see it yours."

"Well, what would he get out of trying anything funny now?"

"On a deal like that? Only the money. And to keep from being crossed himself. Because he couldn't afford to trust anybody."

"How come you know so much about crooked cops, anyway?"

"I've known a couple on the take, they were enough. When I had those three lousy pinball machines paying off. You go help him charge his bank, if there even is one. Maybe you'll go to jail together, if you're lucky."

"There's one thing about you," I said to him, because he was beginning to annoy me, now, with that talk. "You've certainly got plenty of foresight."

"Crut. I've got that, besides hindsight. Get your head out of your can. You need it blown off to believe something? Don't think he wouldn't kill you the first chance he got, if the two of you happened to swing some dumb scene like that. How about when he totaled that half-wit Kenny Sherry and his partner looting the Pig Burger? He fired inside from outside. It wasn't his scene, even. I bet he's got the notches on his piece."

Graemie yawned in the back. "You fellows ring any time you're finished."

"Shut up," Sand-o said to him. "You made a few rocks off the Indian, cool, hombre. Now you think you'll be rich off him. Cop out, man: he look like Santa Claus to you?"

"He isn't an Indian. He was born here."

"Where were they?"

"Oh, funny."

"I forgot, this is buddy week."

"Listen, you can do anything you think you can, Sand," I told him.

"Unquote," Graemie added.

"Oh, brother."

"Well, you want to be paid wages the rest of your life? Have some spotter breathing down your neck?" I said.

"What spotter? You know what you're talking about? Ten years, maybe even the chair. This isn't any pissy-ant fencing bit. You'll be throwing that old thirty-two heat around, with your butt cutting plenty of washers. So if some Enoch moves slow you'll snap off at him. You got to sell out of there fast, then, and pull a big hole over you; while your amigo buddy's off spending the take. Well, later on that bank spieling for me— much later. Because I don't dig your friend Madrid period. Even if I picked up on his angle, which I don't."

"I told you before," I said, "he's sick of the situation out there. He's had it. Did you know he's forty-two? He can't get any decent gig outside of police work because he hasn't done anything else. Hell, not even assembling in an aircraft plant, because he had that trouble here. Unless he becomes a watchman, or ballroom guard. Or rattles doorknobs."

"I wouldn't hire him watching my store," Graemie chimed in.

I went on. "They waived the age limit to get him in out there. They were glad to do it, to get him for seventy-five a week with his background. And then look the other way on the L. A. tough crut. I told you all that. And now this new lieutenant has it in for him, and he can't get anywhere."

"Where's he want to go?"

"That's his work out there."

"What are you, man, his padre?" Graemie cut in.

"Shut up," Sand-o told him for me.

I said, "So he wants to pull this bank thing and get out. He's going to quit and go to Mexico afterward. I know how that talk sounds coming from a heat. I was there. You don't know if you're hearing right."

"Tell me when you are."

"I smell chicken, don't you, hombre?" Graemie said, leaning forward.

"I'll jerk you over your head," Sand-o said to him. "You'll smell something."

"Still chicken," Graemie said.

I came out on the coast highway and went along with it. The traffic wasn't much along the beaches. The sun was lower over the water but enough people were still out. Some had their tents pitched along the old P.E. tracks for the weekend.

That year in Washington had rubbed off on Sand-o more than I'd thought. He was selling estimates for an outfit that sprayed houses with that mastic paint. Except the job didn't last because they used kerosene to thin it. The owner took off somewhere but Sand-o and the paint-gang boss did one for two. Sand-o figured he did the owner's time, so now he didn't trust anybody.

"Watch the car," Graemie tapped me.

I looked. There wasn't any car. Graemie sat back, chuckling to himself.

"Where's this scam bank your friend's got the hots for?" Sand-o asked me. Then I knew he would come around all right.

"He wouldn't say. He wants to get together with us."

"Where?"

"He's asleep in my pad now."

"Isn't that cozy."

"Oh, get off my back, Sand," I told him. "You want to see him?"

"You mean today, don't you?" We'd come almost to Long Beach, just driving along; the oil smell from the wells was blowing towards us.

"Well, why aren't we back there?" Graemie said.

"Because I saw your eyes when I drove up," I told him. But that wasn't true really. Madrid wanted to tell us about it together, but I'd wanted to sound Sand-o first on this part that was a little touchy to bring up.

"I'll take you through what I know," I said to him. "There's no obligation. You and I are supposed to go into this bank. Graemie will be in the car outside."

"Graemie boy? He's un-coordinated."

"He'll be with it."

"Where's the *amigo*."

"Madrid? He'll tell us that later."

"Oh, sure. When he wakes up."

"It's supposed to be set for a Saturday morning. This bank will be closed, like they all are, but there'll be these three clerks working inside. They'll be working on a payroll that has to go out at noon."

"That's where we charge in," Graemie said. "I can see it."

"On horseback," Sand-o said. "Guns fanning."

"You're warm," I told him. "You'll go in first. I'll be up the block with Graemie. When you're inside, we drive up and I come in."

"I'm first." He cleared his throat.

"There's a reason for it."

"I can imagine. Let me guess. All right, so what's on me to get me in the door since I'm first?"

"You go through by osmosis," Graemie said.

"Not quite," I said. "But it's a—psychological—thing."

"A *what?*"

"Well, you know you can ride. You're the only one of us that can, and you're damn good. You come up the street on this horse, then get him to throw you outside the side door of the bank. Don't laugh, yet," I told him.

"Tell me a *scene!* A *horse!* What the hell is *that?*"

"Madrid said we would get it when he explained it. Anyhow, the guard sees it happen through the glass door he's behind. When he sees you lying there in the street he'll come out to help you. Or one of the clerks might. Then you put a gun in the guy's back, leaning against him, and go back inside with him."

Sand-o looked up at the sun visor. He blew through his lips, shaking his head.

"Madrid figures the guard will open up when he sees the accident, because you haven't heard the rest. No one else will be on the street. Now you can laugh," I told him.

He looked at me. "Why should I? What's funny about that? Just me and Old Paint out there." He was blank-faced. "But, just say, for kicks, nobody comes out of the bank?"

"That's where the ace, the psychology comes in," I said; and I hated to say it, all right. "Because then you get up and limp over. And holding your arm. Well, if he hasn't opened the door yet—" and I couldn't say it.

"Don't you dig anything, man?" Graemie butted in. "The old sympathy angle. What a gas. He'll *automatically* help you."

I saw Sand-o's face, then his mouth twist. He reached over the seat and pulled Graemie toward him, holding him by the necktie, and hit him across the face. We were passing a string of oil-well derricks and the slapping was sharp-sounding inside the clanking of those walking-beam pumps. He shoved Graemie back and looked out the windshield, breathing hard.

I heard a snick then and Sand-o turned and I saw Graemie half-standing to use his switch-blade and Sand-o leaning back way up against the dash. Then I was over the white line and a car was in front of me. I threw the wheel over hard, Graemie falling on me as I sideswiped the length of her. I yelled at him but Sand-o had got his wrist. I floored the accelerator to straighten her out and Graemie went back on the seat. Then I heard his knife ripping the upholstery as he cut it into the covers, cursing, and I yelled my head off at him.

"Don't stop," Sand-o told me, white-faced, watching him. I couldn't anyway, because Graemie had fixed himself and I didn't know what he had in his pockets. I cut behind a car to turn onto the crossroad coming and for a bad moment I felt her tipping, then come back. Then we were passing plenty of those oil derricks up on Signal Hill.

When I was sure no car was following us, I pulled

over and got out to look at her. I had black paint swiped along the fender and the bumper end accessory was bent back. There was a deep scratch running along her and the rear fender was creased, but slightly. That was all, and I looked twice. The other car had probably caught the worst part.

Sand-o lit a cigarette; then he took off his jacket, tossing it to me. He knelt in front of the bumper, padding a handkerchief in his hand. He took hold of the end plate and put his foot against the tire. He brought his arm toward him, in slowly, and it was something seeing the accessory straightening. He stopped, dragging on his cigarette, and I looked up. Graemie had gotten out and was walking back up the side of the road.

I caught up to him. "Where you going?"

"Lemme alone."

"Look at your face. You'll get picked up. You want that?" Those oil pumps were walking and hissing around us and I had to raise my voice to hear myself.

"The sonofabitch."

"I'm charging you for my covers."

"Bill that mother."

"You know him. Look how I have to be with him. You know how he is since that." That was why I wanted to break that part to Sand-o, instead of Madrid doing it. Because if you looked at that arm funny he would get a little crazy. None of us ever mentioned it.

"Come on," I told Graemie.

"I'll cut him, hombre."

"You'll have to come back to do it."

He looked down at me. Graemie is six-three and skinny as a rug pole. He wears these shoulder-padded coats that break almost at his knees, and has this hooked nose and pop-eyes and hardly any hair. He's a funny-looking character and is kind of funny. But he just rubs some people at the wrong time.

"Peanut butter," he said, winking at me.

"Gaslight," I told him. It didn't mean anything.

Sand-o stood squinting by the car. He had his jacket back on, with the sleeve shortened the way he wears it, and I could see my bumper plate pulled out from the fender as good as before.

He and Graemie shook hands, though Sand-o kept his right hand in his pocket, using his bad left arm.

EIGHT

The sun was over the rooftops when I parked in my space below. Madrid heard us on the stairs and had the door open waiting inside. We went in and he said hello to Sand-o, and then made Graemie once he saw him. He remembered seeing Graemie in the Lighthouse jazz spot in Hermosa Beach. Graemie used to live over in Hermosa. I didn't know if he was living in town now with all the room-hopping he did.

I'd thought Madrid's car was in a different place downstairs. He'd gone out and bought the pint of bourbon there on the bureau.

"I don't know what you boys drink," he said, "but have some."

No real character drinks much, but Graemie had one. His mouth looked bad, but Madrid didn't ask about it. Sand-o and I took one, then I told Madrid I had passed along everything he'd told me. He had to go soon to make that drive to be at work tonight, and I didn't envy him for it.

He picked at the inside corner of his eye, then sat down at my card table. It was still hot in the room but cooling off now outside.

He had been sitting there, drawing a two-story building with some streets around it. The streets had letters to identify them, and you knew what that building was, standing alone by itself.

Then I recognized where it was. Because he'd drawn a good likeness of this statue of a soldier on a horse, facing what I knew, now, was the bank in the square in his town.

He smiled up at me. "This is Piuma Square, in Cuesta, where I work," he told Graemie and Sand-o.

And I felt cheated. Because I had studied about it, and then put it down. He would know a bank's workings in his own town better than another one, that was likely enough. But they would identify him on sight, too.

"You'd be working close to home," Sand-o said, all right.

"I don't have so far to go," Madrid said, and he grinned. He hooked his arm over the back of the chair, tilting back in it. "Fiesta Day." He took in the three of us. "It ring anything to you boys?"

It didn't to me, nor Sand-o standing next to me. Graemie was sitting slouched sideways on the windowsill alongside the table. He rubbed his nose, his face swollen-looking profiled in the light. But he wouldn't ever win a beauty contest.

"It's a big day, to celebrate the town's founding," Madrid explained. "They hold a parade and a kind of rodeo they call a gymkhana, because they don't use steers or bust any broncs. But they got stunt riders, plenty of big-assed businessmen with fancy saddles to show off, and the uniformed riding club, troops A, B, C, and so on."

I looked at Sand-o, at the same time he did me.

"The streets are lettered alphabetically," Graemie discovered, pointing to Madrid's drawing.

"The town settlers were Mexicanos, so some street names that were too long are changed now. But they're easier to remember alphabetically," Madrid said.

"Wouldn't that bug you," Graemie said.

Madrid smiled. "So everybody that can ride or rent a horse, and has some kind of cowboy outfit, goes in the parade. Then the parade moves out of town, to the riding ring, by eleven o'clock. Everybody goes along in their cars. There's no business in town because it's all closed for the holiday."

I glanced at Sand-o again. But he was listening.

"You boys never know about this goings-on?" Madrid said. "They got no cattle out there, just the citrus ranches and cotton. But they like to have this day."

"You can't ride a lemon," Graemie shrugged.

"It's nothing much to see. But it's in the L. A. papers. Once a year."

"I must have missed it," Sand-o said.

"It's like the celebration they hold in Barstow," Madrid said. "But smaller."

"I don't know what happens in Barstow," Sand-o said, "either."

Madrid's eyebrows came together for a second. "The radio cars go out with the parade," he went on, "to handle the traffic problem and parking." He grinned. "All three of the units we use each shift. One car, extra, is put on the town. Well, I had that detail last year, and I didn't have to ask twice now. It's extra pay, but nobody wants it; you don't get to take in the big thing, the rodeo. I take my night watch, work straight through the extra shift, but don't come in that night."

"Somebody has to watch the town," Graemie said.

"But not the store, eh Graemie?—that your name? I can't go inside with you boys, but I sure can stay south when I have the duty. Because that's when you go in the bank."

"Hold on," said Sand-o. "I'm a little stupid here. Clue a green man, will you? We would hit this bank right after the parade sucks everybody out to the rodeo?"

"You like it, fella?"

"And your part would be *staying away* while we did it?"

"You don't have that guarantee if somebody else is driving the radio car, fella."

"Well, Mary's Hour," Sand-o said. He looked around, shuddering. "I've *heard* it. I think I need a drink."

Madrid's eyebrow twitched. Sand-o went over to the bureau.

"You worry yourself plenty if the uniform unit drives up when you're inside, don't you?" Madrid said over to him. "But with me operating it, you know I don't come."

Sand-o came back, wiping his mouth. He leaned on my card table with his hand, swaying it. "We would be paying for protection, isn't that really it? You'd take no chances, but you'd take the same cut as us, wouldn't you?"

Madrid's eyes were shining. "You got the law *working* with you, Sand-o," he said. "You think about it. You couldn't *buy* that," he went red saying it. "but you got me. And this's something else you don't know about: a World System truck, coming between eleven-thirty and twelve, to pick up the cash payroll, Nick, here, told you about. Well, I guarantee you don't have the truck on you. I promise you don't."

And I could see one of those gray armored trucks, with its gun turrets, showing up while we were inside the bank. I thought Sand-o saw it, too.

"The Sunray is the biggest ranch in the Valley Association," Madrid said, talking slower. "The truck is for them. They can't keep as much cash around, like the smaller ranches. Plenty of Mexican *braceros*— the contract workers—have to be paid for the fruit picking at the Sunray."

"Why can't they be paid off Friday?" Graemie asked.

"On account the payroll includes Friday's picking."

Graemie rubbed his nose. "They can't have this bank deal every Saturday?"

"No, man. The bank takes care of the Sunray, being they're a real big depositor. They extend the service. But regular, the payday is Monday."

"Don't tell me the trouble with Monday." Gaemie looked at the ceiling.

"Monday is Labor Day," Madrid said, grinning. "A national holiday for everybody."

Graemie coughed, faking choking. Then he stopped.

I felt myself tightening up. Because then it would be next Saturday. This Saturday coming. Just eight days away. "You're hard boys to sell," Madrid said. "But I would ask lots more questions myself, you bet."

Sand-o pushed up from the table. He crossed his feet, rubbing his hands on his cords. I could hear somebody talking below on the street.

Madrid picked up his pencil and moved it over his drawing.

"This's the route the World truck takes into town, from El Centro, and the way he goes out to the Sunray. You go in the bank at eleven-twenty and come out eleven-forty, the latest. You got to sack up the vault quick, it's all you got time for. Don't touch the payroll cash."

A fly buzzed in the room and I looked around for it.

"I thought you were handling the truck," Sand-o said to Madrid.

I couldn't get those eight days out of my head. I was seeing the thing clearly, I thought, probably for the first time. Seeing it actually happening.

"I can't hold the truck till Christmas," Madrid said.

"He has to show at the bank by twelve."

I remembered Sand-o's crack about Madrid not being Santa Claus. But that armored truck wasn't a joke.

Just then the old lady came in next door. She slammed the door.

"Crut," I said.

Three of them looked at me.

"Now we get a little piano music," Madrid smiled.

I went to my table by the bed and turned on the radio. I got Larry Finley, the deejay. Graemie snapped his fingers once or twice to the side.

"You'll have a few questions to answer," I said to Madrid, coming over. "They'll have you for lunch afterward, won't they?"

I didn't care about him, though. That was his problem, and he wouldn't have any others.

"A little, no more. I'm in the right spot at the time, see? The World driver likes to shoot a little fat. We're buddy-buddies. He sees me laying along the road, out of service. I got a flat I make, myself. He stops while I change it, and we have a smoke. So the time is shot, eh?"

"What if he keeps going?"

"It's part of my detail to tail him to the bank. He has to wait. The meeting's arranged because he has plenty of cash from previous pickups."

"Oh," I said.

"The department covers me. I don't need no alibi."

"I guess you don't."

"How much would the bank go for?" Sand-o asked, as that piano playing began next door.

"What they keep in a vault? Sixty, seventy thousand, maybe more? This is the only real bank in town, the Security, with all the ranches making deposits. There's a couple Building and Loan, but they're small change. Plenty to go around later, don't worry."

"Where would I get this horse I'm supposed to have?" Sand-o asked him. Madrid knew I'd told him that part.

"The Aurora Stables fix you up, outside town. You got Levis or those cords to wear. Buy a Stetson on the expense account, you'll get it back. Lots of the riders go as masked men; *bandidos*, eh? Buy a mask, too. So they can't remember your face when the horse is picked up."

"You're forgetting something else," Sand-o said. He half-folded his arms.

And I saw the thing getting hot again. But Madrid said, pretty smoothly, "That's why you get a bigger cut. You got the risk with your description. If you don't have to show off your arm, it's still there."

Sand-o stiffened.

"You got to work for your money, too, the hardest. You don't get inside, and everything blows up. We couldn't go without you, for sure."

"How much more?"

"A thousand apiece from us. You buy that?"

I shrugged at Graemie. He licked his puffed-up lips. Madrid hadn't mentioned this cut thing earlier, to me. But I wasn't going to argue about it. If you looked at it, it wasn't any of our money. Still, I was betting he'd just now made it up.

"Why didn't you come see me first-hand?" Sand-o asked him.

"I knew Nick better than you. Not such a good way, it's true. But I didn't know you too good to talk to. Not on this kind of deal."

Well, I've just felt the rug pulled a little, I thought.

Or else I'm listening to a real politician.

"I knew when I got the idea, I had a deal tailor-made for you boys. Hombre and his car, Sand-o for that special business, and somebody for the outside. That's Graemie, here, now."

Move over, Graemie, I thought. You almost have company.

"Why hombre's car?" Sand-o said. And he was pretty bad, I thought. He was pushing it now.

"We got to have a bomb, for one thing. Because you run for the border after the play. You got to be in Mexico in fifteen, twenty minutes, depending how fast you tie the four people up and sack the vault. Then when I roll up behind the World, and you got to beat my call in to the transmitter, be across before that. The border will be the first alerted when the call gets put on the air."

"How far is it to the line?" I asked.

"You know Santa Lucia, just across?"

"I've heard of it."

"You all wait there in this hotel for me, the Cortez. I'll come over when I'm off that night. Then we'll divide up the money. That's the main thing, eh?"

"How far is it?" I said again.

"Twenty-eight and a fraction miles, to the gate."

"Make it—in *fifteen minutes?*" I yelled it at him almost.

"Maybe twenty, hombre. But you can't count on it."

I felt as if I'd been hit. I didn't know what to say.

"You're sure about that fraction?" I said to him.

"I think it's a quarter," he said, set-faced.

"Fifteen minutes clocks you at a hundred twelve, Nick." Sand-o cocked his head at me. "You still got the old Pacers Club shirt?"

"I'll look around," I said. I wanted to sit down.

"You better wear it."

He was damn right I had. I would have to take over from Graemie all right, too. He couldn't get that out of her. I didn't know if anyone could. I looked at Madrid to see if he was kidding at all.

"I was saving it," he said. "It's tough, hombre."

"I'm glad you brought it up," I said to him.

You have everything figured, I was thinking: something for each of the three of us; except yourself. You just let the air out of one of your tires, that's all. But you don't back up for your share.

He took two cards out of his wallet. He wrote a name on one of them with his pencil, then stood up.

"I got a little drive to make, myself, now. I still need the job out there, eh? You boys don't come out later than Tuesday, we'll go over the whole deal good then. Check in this here motel," he said to me. "It's a clean place outside town. Give me a ring right away at the station. Don't leave any moniker, or number. But use this phony name I got here to register. I'll pick up on it."

He gave me the two cards and got his coat. You could hear that piano-playing now with the door open. He stood in the door listening.

"That's *Siboney*, hombre." He flashed his teeth.

"'*Sta bueno*," I said to him.

"Hah, *bueno*." He went out.

I looked at the cards he'd given me. The one for the Desert Star Motel, where he'd written the name I was to use. The other said: Police Department, City of Cuesta, California. Represented by D. M. Madrid.

He'd left his bottle. I went over and took a drink from it.

NINE

Sure, when I'd had my '34 V-8, and I was hooked on drag racing then, that was a different thing. Then I had something modified to do 16 in a quarter-mile, on a drag strip, but she'd cost too much time and money for that pruning.

Now, I told Sand-o, I didn't know if my Ford could do it. Not in the time allowed. And with road conditions to consider.

It was something watching him change in those last few minutes. Graemie'd caught it too.

"Your jalopy's no real beast, O.K. But you don't need any bug-out juice for twenty-eight miles, that's high-gear rolling. That old eliminator you had was always potting out, anyhow," he said.

"Not very often."

"Well, don't get mad. You don't have her anymore. Your Ford winds up pretty tight. The rest is up to you."

"I can drive, Nick," Graemie said from the chair. "In case there's no time to change over."

"I just know her better," I told him. "She fishtails, sometimes, if you don't watch it." Because that was how close it would be. And you couldn't spin the wheels very much and make it. If we could make it at all.

Sand-o went into the alcove and opened the refrigerator. He plugged open two cans of beer. Graemie didn't want one.

Sand-o brought over Madrid's bottle and sat beside me on the bed. "Swig?"

"You go ahead." He took one and chased it with the

beer. "Well, when do we go out?"

"Any time. Before Wednesday."

"What have you got to do?"

"Right now I want to stretch out," I said. "I'm whipped." I was waiting for the two of them to go.

"I have to peddle my bucket of bolts. I'll go over to Washington Boulevard and dump it. You look worried, man. Getting scared?"

"I'm tired," I said. I'll be scared later, I thought; along with you. "I'm talked out and listened out."

"He say anything about pieces to you?"

"I told him you had a collection."

"You would. Well, you keep the thirty-eight. I've got reloads for it, just ask me. I forgot to sound him if I was riding in that dinky parade."

"I don't think you will."

"I can't wear a loaded forty-five with the heat that'll be nosing around."

"I don't expect you'll be in the parade," I said. The fewer people seeing your arm the better, I thought. But it was funny the difference that bonus talk had made in him. And the story Madrid laid on him about having the big role. It might have been true. But maybe he needed that stuff almost as much as the money now, too.

"Well, we're going to rob a bank, man. Is that a blue sky, or isn't it?"

"What are you going to tell your folks?"

"Anything. They'll buy it. The old man is too busy peddling sticks to know what's happening. You know he's opening a store in San Pedro?" Sand-o's father owned a furniture business. "I'll figure out something. Like one of our hunting trips."

"What about Shirley?"

"What *about* Shirley?"

"How about when it's over?"

"We'll be in Mexico. Hell, I'll take one of their Mickey Mouse buses, to Juarez. Come across to El Paso, buy me some wheels, then maybe go to Florida. I want to be long gone when the heat's on so I can spend some loot."

"Whatever it comes to."

"If it's ten thousand apiece, even, it's O. K. Can you beat it for twenty minutes' work? We'll be the highest priced guys in America. What are you planning to do?"

"I have to sit down and think about it."

"Take five, you're down. You should stay down there."

"Where's that?"

"You can talk Mex. You got it made. They won't be able to find you with all the muff hanging on you. Change your loot into pesos and give it back to them with interest."

"We probably won't see each other for a while."

"We can fix something up. Like writing to a General Delivery."

But, with luck, I was thinking, I wouldn't see him or Graemie again. I wondered if he realized how hot his arm was going to make him. It depended how soon they would positively identify him back here. Because they would, sooner or later; then start looking for Graemie and me. I wondered how far I could get before it happened. And if it would be far enough.

"What about you?" I asked Graemie. He was cutting his nails with a clipper, his hands shaking a little.

"Come back here, probably. Play it cool, you know. We shouldn't all drop out of sight, should we?"

Well, you'll be number one, I thought. You're as good

as caught now. So long, Graemie boy.

"Don't forget to turn on your hype friends every night," Sand-o said to him. "Just leave me off your writing list when you're in."

"I'll see you inside," Graemie said. "You'll be there."

"I'd cop out on our pal, Madrid," Sand-o said to me. "You know I would if that action happened."

"You couldn't put him with us. He's alibied pretty good." He took a sip of beer, frowning. "Well, I'm not getting caught. Not in the scene, or any time later. I'm twenty-eight. I'd be thirty-eight when I got out. Maybe forty."

"Don't lose that jinx talk."

"That Indian is putting up nothing. *Nothing*. He'll go back across the border and sleep in his own rack the same night. He can quit and split, then, whenever he wants. He'll have no worry about his heat."

"It's his plan. We wouldn't be doing it without him."

"Without him not helping us. Isn't that a gas? He's promoting the hell out of us. It better come out all right."

"You'll have a big ball in Florida."

"He say anything about Lona on this deal? I didn't want to sound him in front of you."

"I didn't ask him. But he said to call him at the station house. I don't think he'd tell her now, anyway. He didn't when I got rid of that stuff for him."

"Christ, he is a wig, isn't he? I almost forgot about that. I wonder where he took the stuff from. You never know about people, what's inside them. Here he's been a heat all those years. Didn't you get a funny feeling listening to him?"

"I told you."

"Well, I go along with him, on Lona. She's as flap-mouthed as Shirley. You better remember it, too."

"What remember?"

"You told me you clued her about fencing those deals for him. And he looked at you funny there when he said the bank was in his town."

"You ever see a heat look a different way? He knows I was out there, I already told you. He didn't push it because he laid a funny story on me, and I found him out."

"He didn't sound you because he had his bank on his brain. Don't get any more ideas about playing around, in your spare time, buddy-o. Don't flush things for us now."

"Take it easy. I'm not cutting out on you."

"You're sweet. Listen, dig this: what that doctor we knew asked Lona once. How many kids she'd had."

"That weightlifting fixed her up, I guess, didn't it?"

"She's lucky. But know what she said to him? 'I haven't just been sitting on there exactly.'"

"That isn't true." I was sorry I'd said it, then.

"Man, why don't you lend me something? He was a swinging doctor, himself; you know he became a connection later? She used to be ass deep in codeine and bennies every time she came back from his giving her what she said was a cold shot. I think she married Madrid because he was a narco heat—you know? She would think that was a real gas—complete the old goofing cycle for her."

"It would leave her with nothing to shoot for."

"She could divorce him and marry a vice squad fuzz. That'd be too much, man. Listen, when you took the thirty-eight off me, why didn't you say you were going out to see her?"

"I did later."

"Yeah, later."

"You don't have to know everything, do you?"

"You're spooked by that fat greaseball, I know. He impresses you. I could take him with one hand."

You'd have to, I thought.

"You still got eyes for Lona, cop out. I sure don't dig you sometimes. She's been had. I mean but everybody's touched base. Who don't you know? You think of me yesterday?"

"All the time."

"The second time."

"Why don't you lay off before you run down."

He put his beer can and Madrid's bottle on the bureau. "Well, we're just going to charge a little old country store. That's all there is to it. We got four hayseeds inside to handle, then we'll all take that fast ride. I'm talking to him out there, though. See how long he can stall his calling when he gets to the bank."

"You do that."

He mussed my hair. "Take you an hour to comb it, man. You're not really *pachuco*, are you?"

"Where've you been?"

"Where's the blood rays on your hand?"

"They wore off. I'm having a new set."

"See you at Louis' later? We'll talk."

"I'll be by."

"Ay to watcho." It was *pachuco* language for "later." "You going?" he said then to Graemie.

"Go ahead."

"Suit yourself. But keep your hot mouth closed. O. K.?"

"Talk to my can," Graemie said.

"It's an idea. That's where your brains are." He went out taking the steps noisy, two at a time.

"He'll be all right," I said to Graemie.

"I don't give one. He doesn't bother me."

"I'll let you have the thirty-eight, if you want. He just wanted you to ask him for a piece."

"I can latch onto one."

"It'll save you the trouble. I'll get another off him, with his arsenal."

"You got anybody to tell, Nick? That you'll be gone for a while?"

"Just Mrs. Flores, that I used to live with. I think she might be married again since her husband died."

"Who's she?"

"She used to be my guardian, sort of."

"What happened to your folks, hombre?"

"They were killed in a car accident."

"I never knew that. You pick up Spanish off this Mrs. Flores?"

"No, she's Greek. She was a friend of my folks. Her husband was Mexican."

I'd known Graemie a few years. But for all his joking at times, he was pretty private. He never talked about himself that I could remember. He was the only real character among us, too. I think you have to be born one to really be one.

"You goofing much?" I asked him. He was looking jumpy.

"With my will power, man?" He raised his eyebrows.

"Well, take it easy, anyhow."

I went over and watched him come out of the entrance below. He crossed the street, cutting through the Fresno Market parking lot. A girl looked around at him, he was that tall and skinny, funny-looking. Then a car backfired starting, and I could see him jump from all the way up here.

I stretched out on the bed. It had been a long day, it seemed. The day that's going to change your life, next week, I thought. That's what kind of a day it's been.

I lay awhile with my radio turned off, watching it get darker outside. The parking lot lights came on from the market, lighting a section of the ceiling. I could hear the old lady next door fixing dinner on her hotplate with her door open. *Siboney*, I thought. She must have had some older pupils taking lessons from her.

Some kids came by in two cars, yelling, downshifting for the corner stop sign. Then it was quiet for a while. I heard the old lady washing her dishes in the bathroom sink. When she put on her television I got up and went out to eat.

TEN

Over the weekend I cleaned up a few things. I saw the manager of the building Sunday morning playing the hose out front. I told him I would be out of town for a couple of months and was giving up my place. He had two girls in line to move in and I told him I would be out by Tuesday. Then I got a call on the ad I'd put on the Fresno Market bulletin board. I picked up a trailer and pulled my studio bed over to the Crenshaw Center. This chiropractor was there to open his office and give me the ten dollars. He didn't want my chair I'd brought along, but I threw it in anyhow. The building manager loaned me a box spring and mattress to sleep on.

Monday I went to the Richfield office in L.A. and paid my bill from the gas slips I had in my wallet. I came back to town and settled the balance I was carrying at Harris's haberdashery. I stopped by the phone company and cut off the service, then I left my collection of paperbacks and magazines at the Goodwill. I couldn't think of anything else I had to do.

We had seen plenty of people Saturday night, when Sand-o and I made the rounds. Sand-o had the money from selling his Olds and sprung me to several beers. We dropped it we were going along the Rogue River in Oregon for a camping and hunting trip. Sand-o was starting a blond beard, as if he wouldn't be shaving where we would be. We said Graemie was going with us, but he wasn't around. By Monday night, we were out looking for him.

There was a fog blowing from the ocean, and I was

driving back in it late, from Long Beach. We had looked for Graemie earlier in town. But he didn't hang out much at the regular spots except Louis'. And he had some friends we didn't know about.

We came back into town and you couldn't see the tops of the palms along the boulevard. Then, driving past the Alcazar Motel, we made a red-and-white Dodge convertible in the driveway with its parking lights on. Ray Magallanes, a pusher, had one like it. I thought I would wait by the Dodge and ask Magallanes if he had seen Graemie.

Sand-o came with me. We went up the driveway and there was a single light on the second floor. Someone was playing bongos low up there but they carried. I thought I would go up and listen outside. You could tell Magallanes' funny, high voice.

We came around the corner of the motel office, and Graemie was there in the shadows.

He was leaning over a soft-drink cooler, chopping the ice inside with a pick. He had some pieces in a towel on the folded-back bottom of the cooler lid.

"Greetings," he said to me.

"We've been looking all over for you. We're going out tomorrow."

"Today," Sand-o said. It was after three.

"Let's go, then," Graemie said to us.

He was straight enough on junk not to even recognize us.

"What's the ice?"

"Big party upstairs." He went on chopping in the cooler, splashing water.

"Who's drinking?" I asked him.

"Man, broom off. Can't you see I'm preoccupied?"

"Let's go," Sand-o said to him.

Ray Magallanes was coming down the outside stairway. Magallanes was a sawed-off, big-talking character. He had a girl behind him, and this *pachuco* gorilla Machaquito, called Apache, he ran around with. Apache wore a purple suede jacket and sandals, and had sideburns almost to under his chin. The girl was one of the prettiest Mexican girls I'd seen.

Magallanes nodded to us and the three of them got in the Dodge. We let them back up past us. Then we started down the driveway with Graemie in tow. Then this car, that must have been parked there at the curb, jumped across the driveway behind Magallanes. Magallanes jumped out of the Dodge and quick threw something away from him. One of the guys coming out of the blocking car, a Ford, trained a light on Apache. Then the driver came up to the left side of the Dodge, flashing a light on Magallanes and the girl.

We hustled Graemie behind the office. I didn't think we'd been seen in the action.

You could hear the one guy talking to Magallanes, and the girl going on fast in Spanish as they got out of the Dodge; and the heat saying keep your voice down shut up clue her in Mex to Magallanes. Then it was quieter, and I knew the heat was shaking Magallanes. He couldn't touch the girl.

I could hear the motel manager snoring next to us with his window partly open and all these big millers were smacking noisily into the neon vacancy sign over the driveway. Then the shadows crossed in front of us, going away, and I heard a car start, the Ford. I made the Dodge's door squeaking open but not closing, and it being rolled down the driveway and started out in the street.

Sand-o went up and looked around the corner of the office. He came back and took a cigarette off me.

"Another sedan's double-parked out there. Christ, it's foggy. I think Magallanes and his friends are in the back seat. They have the Ford backed up along the curb. One of the heat's behind the wheel."

"The other must be clouting Magallanes' Dodge."

"They'll turn a spike outfit in it."

"They saw us drive up. Can you see out to the car?"

"Hell no."

We had a kilo of marijuana stashed behind the spare, that was what we had gone to Long Beach for. Besides, we had three .38's, a .380, a .32, two .45's, an M-1, a Winchester, a Springfield, and all those shells in the trunk. We wouldn't be coming back from Cuesta so Sand-o had taken most of the pieces he wanted with him.

Graemie turned around and leaned over the ice cooler, groaning. "Hold his head under water," Sand-o said.

"How many are in your party?" I asked Graemie.

"What party?" There you were, all right.

You could hear jazz playing, on a record, probably, up there now, this sax climbing. Graemie looked awful, then I realized it was that sick blue light from the motel sign. But he looked bad, his eyes glazed up and hardly any pupils.

"We won't be seeing Magallanes for a while," Sand-o said. "I mean, nobody will."

"We'll see him if they break into my trunk. There's no way out back there, either." The Alcazar is built in a double-decked horseshoe and you have to come out through the front. There's a back door through a tunnel but it was kept locked after this knifing happened in the tunnel.

Then a car started and drove off. I went up to look and came back. "Nothing's out there, now. Either car. The heat that made the pinch must be going in to the booking office."

Just then Graemie began throwing up into the cooler. He was tearing his head off and I thought the manager inside would wake up, with his window half open.

We waited for Graemie to stop because it was the dry variety. He had thrown up probably when he'd shot up. I went to have another look up front. And then I came back.

"They're working in teams. They want all the fish, all right. A Ford's pulling into the same spot the other was in. Three heat in it," I told Sand-o. We had Graemie to thank for keeping us from walking right into them.

"They'll raid soon," Sand-o said.

Graemie pulled himself up, skinny and stoop-shouldered. He was shaking, just that stringy stuff hanging from his mouth.

"Can you stop it?" I asked him.

He shivered. He smelled, and his suit looked like he was sleeping in it steady.

"No more, hombre. Gut's busted. Where's Maggy?"

That was Magallanes. "He's faded," I said.

"— with him, and Apache."

"How many pads you hit tonight?"

"Two days. Running. Celebrating leaving, you know? Maggy's coming back for me."

"Did you shoot up upstairs?"

"In the car. Maggy's spike."

"Maggy won't be back for you."

"You think I'm gonna make it?" he asked me. He

looked rough enough to spook you.

"I wouldn't give odds on you," I told him.

I shut the cooler lid and tapped on the window with my ring. You could see the manager inside on a cot, in his undershirt and trousers. He wouldn't wake up. Then I hit the bell, once, and he swung a leg over the side of the cot. He came to the window.

I paid him for a double and signed a phony name on the clipboard he shoved out. He gave me the key. The room was above the office, to the left.

We went in, and I moved a chair into the bathroom for Graemie. I shut the door on him. Then Sand-o turned off the light above us.

We looked out the front window through the venetian blinds. It was practically a grandstand seat.

Nobody had touched my car, where I'd left it on the other side of the driveway. The heat behind the wheel of the green Ford below now was talking into the mike. The one next to him was writing something by flashlight. Another sedan was parked a few cars behind, with the front right door open. The two heat from it were playing their flashlights around the front yard of the real-estate office next door. It was where Apache had thrown the goodie he had on him. The hype party was in the back of the motel, so the heat were taking their time looking. You could hardly see them, it looking creepy with their flashlights showing in the fog swirling around.

The three heat were getting out of the first Ford now. One of them had his revolver out. He put it back in his pants. Then one of them put his hand in the back of the car and helped a matron out I hadn't seen in there.

We went to the door, opening it a little. They were

going up the stairs, then tiptoeing along the balconied hallway. The matron brought up the rear. They ganged up outside the party door and the lead heat listened, then knocked. I figured Magallanes had copped out on the knock the hypes were using.

The door opened, and the three heat went in.

Somebody was knocked down, or fell, in the action. Then I saw it was this character sitting on the floor with his bongo drums between his legs, and there was all the shouting. I heard a door inside being kicked, and you knew it was to the head, then someone slammed the front door. But you could hear some yelling still plainly.

We looked out the window, then. And three prowl cars had driven up below.

They all came out in around twenty minutes. There were nine fellows, and three girls. I recognized a couple of the heads. The ones the heat had probably had to wake up walked along the hallway like sleepwalkers. One of the girls was staggering and lipping off to the heat about it being her birthday. The rest were quiet though.

A few hypes got in the narcos' two cars and the rest piled into the radio cars. The matron got in one of the cars after the girls. They all went off, then, leaving the two heat there looking for Apache's goodie next door.

Sand-o and I stretched out on the double bed. We put a quarter in the radio to drown out Graemie's moaning still in the bathroom.

We decided to leave my Ford where it was. It was safer now, anyway, in front of the motel. We had our clothes in it, also. But I had a picture of Madrid when he found out we were busted and in the joint, with those scenes in my Ford's trunk. We couldn't come any closer and not make it next time.

We lay awake for a while talking, and a tow unit came and went twice for the hypes' cars that were parked below. We listened to its call radio and hoist winch rattling.

I woke up with the light on my face, coming through the blinds. And there were the three of us in bed, Graemie having crawled over in the middle.

We were the three musketeers, all right.

ELEVEN

I pulled into the Desert Star Motel, off the highway leading into Cuesta, around four o'clock. There were half a dozen big palms lining the gravel driveway back to the motel, which had five cabins on each side. It was a run-down place, with a café that served beer and wine in front and had benches and a horseshoe throw around the side.

After we registered, Sand-o and Graemie using aliases too, I called the station house from the café. I asked for Madrid, but I didn't leave a message. Then we brought our gear in, but left the guns locked in the trunk. There was no cleaning service, but we didn't trust the fat woman managing the place not to come in. When we were in, I pulled the car up close to the door and locked it.

We were sitting in the café about five-thirty, with one of the big floor fans blowing toward us, drinking beer. The fat woman who ran the motel came in the back door. She had a phone call for Ralph Williams, that was me. Madrid was on the ball, I thought. She sat down at the bar and I went out to take the call in the office.

Madrid had phoned in to the station when he got up, and they told him someone had called. He wanted us to meet him at a place called Rialto Pass. He said it was the last signpost as we came in. I remembered seeing it. He wanted us to be there at seven.

We got in the car after we ate at the café, and Madrid passed us in his Plymouth, on the highway going out. I followed him into the Rialto Pass turn-off.

We passed a couple of forked roads with RFD boxes at the turn. We were climbing gradually, then it began to get steeper. We came into a back canyon, winding through it, past a spring running under the road through a pipe. Then Madrid turned up sharply, onto a spur going off. The dust he put up half hid him. But he didn't climb very high, coming out then suddenly on this mesa.

He drove around a burned-out house fronting on the cliff side and stopped. I stopped on the other side of the foundation.

Someone bad gone to a lot of expense and trouble to build the house; running a bulldozer up to cut the hill down and hauling everything else up. Only the big stone fireplaces were standing now, and there wasn't firewood left. But plenty of beer cans and trash in the weeds.

Then you saw the spring, running down the hillside fast through the brush, that had been dammed so it made a waterfall spilling over the cliff to below where we'd passed it. And there was no doubt about the view.

Madrid waved us to the edge of the cliff. He had a pair of field glasses.

"I didn't know if to expect you boys today for sure. I thought maybe you cooled off a little."

"We took it easy coming out," I said.

"I was joking. I wanted to show you the town from up here. It's the best place for us to meet, I think. The lovers don't show up till late."

"What happened to the house?" Graemie asked.

"It burned up being built. Tough, eh? Don't count your chickens, you never know. The driveway wasn't laid, yet. It's kept cleared for a fire trail in case the brush goes up, back down there."

I looked at Rialto Pass directly below us. It was a shortcut into town, saving about four miles of the right-angling highway. If you didn't care about climbing up and around the curves.

Madrid pointed out the stables and riding ring where the rodeo was held. I looked at them through the glasses, across town and a few miles beyond some yellow-white cotton fields. The wooden stands around the big ring were tiered several rows up and there was a roofed grandstand. There was a big parking space before the ring.

There were trails cleared in the hills behind the stables, Madrid said. The riding clubs were a big thing because there wasn't much of anything else around. You couldn't hunt back in the small box canyons if there had been game in them. And the nearest sizable body of water, for sports, was the Salton Sea to the north.

Then the hills ran out, and I turned the glasses to the mountains beyond. I could see the desert sand-hills in between, dead kite and gray now, looking like heaps of sifted ashes in the light there was left.

The three of us passed the glasses for the bank. It was a two-story pink stucco building, with a sidewalk arch built out for the sun. Madrid described the inside as we studied the outside.

We looked at the route we would take afterward, beginning with the street behind the bank. But the far hillside blocked off the rest of the country toward the border. It was a narrow two-lane road all right, but with the citrus ranches touching it all the way to the quarantine strip on the map Madrid had sketched in my room. As well as I could see, there was nothing out there that would slow us up.

Madrid pointed out the place below in the Pass where he would meet the World armored truck. The truck would take that route to escape the parade and rodeo traffic that would be crossing the highway at the time.

He said he would meet us at the Pass the next afternoon, and take us in town in his car, to show us the inside of the bank. But he was going to phone us at the motel first, to check. Then he left. We saw him come out below, then head down the Pass. The lights were coming on in town now, and we left after a few minutes.

We sat in the cabin for an hour, playing gin rummy. We finished with Graemie small winners. The television was free, but not worth watching. The signals on the couple of stations you could get were too weak.

Madrid wanted me to keep my car away from town. Just in case any of the other cops might still remember its description. That liquor store man outside Imperial hadn't caught my number, so she wasn't really hot. But Madrid wanted to play it close.

So there wasn't anything much for us to do. I got my trunks out and went up to where the gravel driveway between the cabins ended at a wooden stairway going up to a set-back pool. That wasn't much more than a cemented melon wash.

No one was up there now. Four of the cabins had cars in front of them, but the rest were empty from earlier. Sand-o sat by the pool in one of the faded, bird-crutted canvas chairs, his cigarette sparking in the dark. Graemie stayed in the cabin. Graemie was a buddy, but he was still a junkie. He had that bunk habit of junkies. Then we came down and woke him up and we went up to the café in front.

It was hot inside with the two big fans going. It was sticky, muggy, for near-desert country. Sand-o took off his jacket, hanging it over his arm. He could handle himself most of the time so you wouldn't notice that shortened sleeve. Then he began to get a little along, and became sore having to sit like that, or close to the table. He took two bottles of beer out to the benches alongside the café. He came in a moment later, and asked me for the car keys. He wanted to get the grass in the trunk for a poke.

I sat at the table with Graemie, who wasn't the best conversationalist when there wasn't a bunch around. He dummied up when you were alone with him. He hadn't waked up dry-mouthed, but you couldn't drink more than a couple with him because he wasn't interested in the stuff anymore.

After a few minutes, he went over to the bar for change to play the shuffleboard table.

I leaned my chair against the wall and took in the handful of people at the bar. A kid couple from the motel were arguing at one of the tables. The girl looked high on wine.

I was thinking about Saturday. But wondering if it wasn't something else about the three of us. The bank had us edgy enough, and scared, all right. Besides the run to the border, and what would come after. But it was almost as if each one of us was for himself, now. And the feeling had been growing on me practically from the start.

Madrid was the outsider. We couldn't fully trust him, or he trust us. That was bad thinking, itself. But it was true, and we couldn't help the setup. But what I was thinking went beyond that; or before. Because maybe the three of us had one or two things in common, and there never was anything else: we were strangers. Maybe there was nothing outside of the Goodnight, Saxie's and Louis'; past playing buck dice for drinks and scoring for grass now and then. Nothing after closing the spots and the drive-ins, but only those things in themselves. That's what I was wondering, now, with Sand-o having gone outside, and Graemie stooped there over the shuffleboard. And the three of us going into town on Saturday.

Then I considered it further. Probably the trouble lay with ourselves, originally, in our thinking. Because if there was any real basis for it in the things we did have, we would have been that closer way right now. But that was how it was. You lived the way you thought. And I thought about that a little. And I made it, finally, the hell with the past. There was never any more time for going back. Because there never was time enough for the future.

I kicked my chair down and went up to the bar. Graemie came over for change and went back to the shuffleboard. Then I decided, what did I care, I would tell Sand-o later. Because I didn't want to argue with him now. What was he to me anyway? And he would be less after Saturday. He would be nothing then. And Graemie, too. We were all waiting for the time to pass. That was one thing the three of us always had.

I went to the phone booth by the stockroom in back. I looked up the motel's number, then checked Madrid's. It was almost eleven and he would be reporting in at work.

It took Lona a minute to answer. She had got out of bed.

"Well, it's nice of you to call."

"I rang you twice on Friday night, and Sunday night."

"I wasn't home."

I put my hand over the mouthpiece to hear her better.

"I feel rotten," she said.

"Do you want me over there?"

"Oh, surely. Right now."

"I'm out here."

"You're where?"

"At a motel. The Desert Star."

"You're staying *here?*"

"I can't talk longer now," I said. "Take down this number. I'll wait." She came back. "Ask for Ralph Williams. I'm using an alias here." I gave her the number of the motel.

"Are you in trouble?"

"No."

"I don't understand it."

"My not being in trouble?"

"That, too."

"You don't have to."

"Play your little games."

"Just call me back, Lona."

"I'll call you."

I came back inside to the bar. Graemie had moved over to the Skee-Ball machine. I picked up my bottle of beer and went out the back door and passed the side. Sand-o was on one of the whitewashed benches. He had his jacket hung over the back rest. You couldn't see his runt arm in the darkness. He was holding a cigarette with that hand. It wouldn't be a joint, I knew. Besides I couldn't smell it. He'd probably turned on already in the cabin.

I sat beside him.

"They'd bug me after a week in this hole," he said. "Both of us."

"Our fuzz friend, Madrid, just drove past. He saw me sitting here. He blinked his lights."

"Oh? Maybe something's come up."

"Like what?"

"How would I know?"

"He'd call up, wouldn't he?"

"I guess he would."

He butted his cigarette against the heel of his boot and stood up. "I don't like to be checked up on. That's all he's doing." He walked up to the horseshoe pit.

He threw a few shoes. One of them sparked off the peg ringing.

I finished my beer. "Ready for another?" I asked him. A truck slammed by on the highway. I didn't hear his answer. Just then the fat landlady came out of the office. She turned toward the cabins, then saw us. "Telephone, Williams," she yelled over.

I looked at Sand-o. It was pretty funny, all right.

I went in the office and took the call from Lona. I told her I'd meet her in ten minutes. As I came out Sand-o was coming out the back of the café. He had his jacket on, carrying two bottles of beer. He set them on the bench.

"I was getting those," I said.

"Don't lay something on me for nothing. What did he want?"

"He wants me to meet him at the Pass. He said to bring a couple of beers and we'll talk. It's quiet for him tonight."

"Like when isn't it."

"That'll be Saturday."

"Not for him. Well, don't let me keep you. You're the group leader."

I didn't answer him. I went in the café and bought four bottles of Miller's. Graemie was sitting at the end of the bar, by the wall. He had a wine and soda in front of him. With his black suit and tie he looked like some stranger in there. He was, all right.

I told him I was meeting Madrid. I went out and left him sitting there looking lost, hunched over on the stool, two hundred miles from his street corners.

I walked back with Sand-o to the cabin. He was going to try and watch the television. I left two of the beers with him and got in the car. I drove out, past the big, still palms along the gravel driveway, and the racket coming loud outside from the café's juke.

TWELVE

The town square was deserted, dark except for the night lights in the stores and the streetlights. I drove around the statue of the horse soldier and slowly past the bank building. An iron gate was pulled across the front entrance. To the side was the stairway door to the law firm on the second floor. There were several names gold-lettered on the four windows above the sidewalk overhang. On the right side of the building was a parking lot and then stores to the end of the block.

I turned the corner and drove past the side entrance we would go in. There were the two wrought-iron-and-glass doors Madrid had drawn for us. A light was burning somewhere inside the bank. I circled the block, passing the street we would take to hook onto the border road. Then I swung back across the square and out into the streets of the tract where Madrid lived.

The light in the living room went out as I came down the block. Only a few other houses had their lights on.

Lona came down the walk. I opened the door for her.

"I could hear your pipes five minutes ago."

"Your neighbors go to bed early." I drove ahead slowly, though.

"Now tell me what this is all about. Then I have something for you."

"It's a long spiel," I said. "What were you saying?"

"I don't feel like being funny, getting up."

"I remember."

"I looked through all the old papers we have in the carport, saving them for the Community Chest. It was a chore. There's a Davidson's discount store on B Street. Their warehouse was broken into about a month ago. A whole bunch of things were taken. It was in the paper."

"Well," I said, "that's old news, still."

"You're so appreciative. That's the thanks—"

"He's been in to see me again. He practically admitted thieving that stuff. Listen, don't you want to know why I'm out here?"

"Yes. I do."

It was a kick glancing at her as I drove, and talked. The expressions kept tumbling over one another.

After I was through talking, she'd had it. I gave her a cigarette and punched the dash lighter. I was driving slowly, idling almost, past some hay fields. The smell of the clover came strong without a breeze.

"When you said he asked you to fence some things, I still didn't believe it. Maybe I didn't want to. Until I saw that in the paper."

"You'll read about this in headlines."

"That was on the front page, out here."

"They'll have an extra this Saturday."

"You three, and him. Robbing the Security Union. I'm glad I don't have much money in there." Then she realized it.

"You'll get it back," I said. "At a thousand per cent interest."

"He wants to go to Mexico later," she repeated. She blew smoke into the dash lights.

"It's your chance to get out of this tom place."

"I've wondered about him lately. I've been the queen of the island these past few days. With him knowing you'd been out here. But he never said anything to me."

"I don't think he would. Even if he knew."

"Are you ever dreaming."

"He is. About his bank."

"I can't get over it. And Sand-o and Graemie in it. Why are you going into it, Nicky?"

"Money."

"I guess ask a silly question."

"You don't think that's the answer?"

"Not all of it."

"It's the best offer I've had. I'm not working anymore. I'm tween jobs."

"Tell me something new, Nicky."

"I won't have that trouble after Saturday."

"Where are you going?"

"I haven't decided, yet."

"I mean now. Let's go and sit somewhere. You can buy me drink."

"Does he ever go by the house or come in, when he's on duty?"

"I've never known about it. He may drive past. But I always have the lights out after I go to bed."

"There's two Miller's in this sack, if you want one."

She pushed the glove compartment button and got the opener. I stopped to open the bottles and toss the sack out. She put her bottle on the ledge the glove compartment door makes open. I put mine there after I took a swallow. I listened to the engine running a little uneven.

"We brought some grass out. A kilo."

"Where is it?"

"At the motel."

"That's what I need to pick me up. I've been feeling

poorly."

"What's the matter?"

"My system's upset, the doctor says. He gave me some pills. They total you. That's why I was sleeping when you called."

"I'm on your side. You look fine to me."

"Oh, sure. Getting up, flying out of the house like this." She had on a black corduroy jumper over a pink blouse. She nearly always wore those small button-kind of earrings. These were pink.

"Let's go out to the motel. I'd like to see Sand-o and Graemie anyhow."

"I don't want to chance it. He went by a while ago in the radio car."

"We shouldn't be driving around. We could run into him, anywhere."

She turned in the seat and had her shoe off. She put her foot under her. The slip she wore underneath showed, rustling. I put my hand behind her head and leaned over and kissed her. I put my arm around her waist and held her closer. She put her fingers inside mine and I kissed her again. She turned her head and brought her mouth back across mine, then held my hand against her cheek and looked at me.

"Where can we go?" I said.

"If it was earlier, we could drive across to Santa Lucia. Your clock isn't working."

I looked at my watch. "It's eleven-thirty."

"We couldn't make it across the line and back by twelve."

"Can we score some maryjane over there?"

"Can you. I drove over once in a while."

"He says you can put it down."

"He never picked it up really. But we couldn't score

and get back before they shut the gate. It closes at midnight and doesn't open till six."

"What time does he get in in the morning?"

"About seven-fifteen."

"We could stay over and be back before then."

"We couldn't make the gate now, Nicky."

"I have to make that run Saturday. In fifteen minutes. This is a good time to try dry-running it. I can make it in half an hour easy."

"What time is it?"

"Eleven thirty-five."

"It will take you ten minutes to get on the border road."

"I'll try it from the square. Then the conditions will be the same as the real scene. Except the action will be in daylight."

"I don't want to drive like that. Night or day."

"I remember somebody who would try anything once."

She looked at the two bottles of beer. She hadn't touched hers. She held her chin, thinking. I said something but she didn't listen. She always went far away when she got like that. She looked pretty there in the glow from the underneath dash lights.

"He's crazy you can do it in fifteen minutes."

"I can find out if he is."

"Will you stop if I ask you?"

"I'll know before then. We'll toss these out." I took a quick drink. I opened the door, leaning out, and rolled the bottles under. They rolled gurgling in the dirt.

"There's a waste."

I was turning the car around. "We'll have two cold ones in Mexico."

THIRTEEN

I came back through the hay fields, past the stacked bales that smell like manure, and got up on the road. Then I headed for the business district.

Coming into the square, the exhaust racketed off the stores and low buildings. I braked, going into a second-gear skid, making the S-turn onto the street behind the bank. There were cars parked outside some of the houses, but it was a wide street, with room enough to pass.

Then I saw the big dip ahead, too late, and couldn't touch the brakes. She left the paving and hit hard. She swerved toward the curb and I slapped into second, power-spinning her, then she righted back.

"Are there more of those things?" We were rocking, the curb warners scraping the road. Lona had her hand against the dash, sitting sideways, holding the back of the seat. She shook her head.

I cut onto the border road. The wind was blowing past the wind wings, and the dash lights had gone out when we'd hit after the dip. I put the accelerator down to the floor. I had a gyp floormat with universal pedal holes. The air getting through blew the dust off it.

Headlights were coming toward us.

"Is there any rough part to this road?" I said. "Holes or washboard?"

"I never hit any," Lona answered. She reached behind her and rolled up the window.

"I hope we don't."

The car began pulling off to the shoulder. As we

passed its horn blared. I hoped nothing had happened up front when we'd hit. If an oil line came loose she would throw some rods.

I hit the high beam and rode the middle of the road. It was unlighted except for the main gates of the ranches; but straight as a line. But I wished for more moonlight. There were the ranches on the sides, all along, going far back, and the lights outside the field workers' compounds, and the night was turned cool now with the speed-wind.

I passed a few cars coming and they were wind slaps. I had the accelerator opened up since we came onto the road. Now we could see the glow rising that was the border town, Santa Lucia.

I tripped the lights and picked up a truck ahead. It had a flickering white taillight. I rode the wrong side of the road to pass it. It seemed as if it was slowing down. A car was standing toward me, out beyond my high beam, its lights pin-pointing. And then bright lights. I put mine down.

I hit the button again. The car's high lights were blinding me. I couldn't find the truck to pass it. I couldn't see any flickering taillight in the glare. The car flashed its lights for me to get over. Then they went out. And it was the truck blocking them, turning across the road.

I swung over, trying for the edge of the asphalt. We were doing a hundred, and I didn't want to touch the dirt shoulder, I didn't know what was out there. I hit the brakes, punching them, the tires sounding like something ripping, and felt the shuddering go through her, and I ducked as the windshield post cleared the back of the truck.

I passed the oncoming car wide open, still swaying.

She took it all at once with no smell of gas. I put her ears back again, then I pinned them back. Nothing was coming or going, and I was thinking about that truck. She turned up high-sounding as routed metal whining, all out but not flatting, still trying. I took her that way, way out beyond the headlights, then I looked over at Lona, who hadn't moved or made a sound, and grinned. If we were going to make it now we would.

I was coming up to the border gate. It was still up, the floodlight masts throwing long shadows. A customs inspector was sitting on a chair on the walk between two driveways. I let her run down. The inspector picked up the chair, heading for the office on the side. I put on speed for the last fifty yards, pulling into the driveway. I blew the horn. One of them looked out of the office window. Then he waved me across. The Mexican inspector ahead waved me past.

As we went over I heard a noise behind. I looked back. The gate was lowering on its wheels.

"Now we'll get those drinks."

"I'll need the bottle."

"You're a co-driver, all right."

"I was too scared to say anything. I want out of this car. Don't look for a place."

I stopped outside a bar. The sidewalk curbs were a foot and a half high. I took Lona's hand and we went inside the café. A woman was tending the bar. We took the back booth, that was half-blocked with beer cases.

We sat together on the one side. The air coming in the opened back door smelled of chickens. The woman came out from the bar. I told her two margueritas.

Lona's hand shook holding the stemmed glass. Both

of my hands stung. The insides of my fingers were red and blistering from holding the wheel. I'd opened an old callus and it had bled a little.

"How fast were we going?"

"I couldn't see the speedometer. She'll do a hundred fifteen true, or used to. Anything over that we picked up."

"I feel like I'm riding, still. My insides are shaking."

"The new cars will all break a hundred and some. Now they have the factory horsepower. But you have to take off for the speedometers. They aren't right."

"I'll have another."

"You're moving fast."

"I learned off your driving."

I took the glasses to the bar and brought two more back. "Where's the action in this town?" I wondered out loud. A dirty white chicken was wandering around out in the back. The men in the place looked like working men, wearing caps, and drinking in the booths without women.

"We have all night. Don't come on like gangbusters."

We came out, and a few taxis were going by, cruising for fares. The air had a night smell but was dusty still. The wide drag was blacktopped in the middle, and the rest unpaved and rain-holed to the high curbs.

A few liquor stores had their signs lit besides the handful of cafés. Groups of three and four Mexicans were hanging around the darkened store fronts the way they do.

I started the engine and lifted the hood. I got the flashlight and poked it around listening to her. She was hot but running all right. I closed the hood and pulled out and drove up the drag.

"Which way is the Cortez Hotel?"

"How do you know that?"

"It's where we're meeting him here, after the play."

"We'll see it. There aren't any other hotels or motels in town."

"Sounds like a real town."

"Well, it's no Tijuana, or Mexicali. But it has its places. We turn up here."

I drove up the dirt side street. None of them seemed to be paved off the main drag. I stopped outside the El Charro Café, next door to a combination liquor-grocery. It was all file-parking. You couldn't open a door alongside those high rain curbs. The characters in front of the store eyed Lona as we went into the café.

Inside it was dark, with only the light from the back-bar. Lona introduced me to the bartender. He made us two margueritas. I let her do the talking, in Spanish. She asked him where this José was, who was going to score for us. He went to a curtain at the end of the bar and put his head through it. A big, good-looking dark Mexican in a waiter's monkey jacket came out. I shook hands with him. He stood next to Lona and had a shot of tequila. She asked me for ten dollars to give him. Then he took off his white jacket and put it in one of the empty booths.

"He wants to use the car."

"I'll take him where he's going."

"He's very careful. Give him the keys, don't be one-way."

"You know what I have in the back." I had told her about the pieces.

She told him I would drive him then. I went out with him.

He was a good friend of Lona's, he said. He was glad

to score for me because the town wasn't cool for some things to strangers.

I drove up a string of back streets until he had me stop outside a line of tarpaper shacks. He went around the back of them and I cut the engine. I listened to the crickets rubbing their wings in the grass. A dog with mange sores came up and growled up at me. It was swelled out with pups. I hit the door with my hand and it ran off. Chickens were clucking somewhere in back of the shacks.

This José came out and laid two brown-paper-wrapped rolls of marijuana on the seat. I put them in the glove compartment. He got in and I started the engine, then turned around.

"You have papers?"

"I was going to ask you."

"Don't try to buy. You use your cigarettes, O.K.?"

"Why?"

"These people hang around the cafés no good. They don't want to work. A few are O.K. But some think you make a buy, and give your license to the border. When you go across you get stopped. They get a reward for what you carry. You tell where you get it, I go to jail here."

"That's how it is."

"I go to jail twice. No good." He waved his hand. "I spend from now on keeping out."

"The people who grow the stuff take a chance."

"They are whores, most of them—girls get too old to work. They steer tourists into the houses, or sell the rubber things—the crazy ones, you know—or grow *grifa*. The police don't bother, unless the border asks them—the U.S. side. They shut down the gate and the town is dead. All the business."

"I haven't seen much."

"You don't been to the Zumbido?"

"What's that?"

He grinned. "The business section. Lona can show you."

"Who showed her?"

"I showed."

"How long do you know her?"

"Over a year. She is very pretty. A little Spanish-looking. You, too, but not Spanish. You speak?"

"Some."

"You know Lona long?"

"Over a year," I said.

"You know her husband? No good."

"Why not?"

"No *policia*." He turned his thumb down.

"He's not a good policeman."

"No policeman any good. I do favors for Lona. For you, now, too."

"Thanks."

"No trouble, man."

"We'll have a drink," I said.

We were back at the café and went in. Lona was sitting in one of the booths. A Mexican girl was talking with her. I told this José to bring us a round. He put on his white jacket and got his tray. The girl had a shot of pulque, and José stood having his tequila shot. Then we told them so long and we went out.

"Who's that Rosita?"

"She's a barfly. She tricks sometimes for drinks."

"Where's this Zumbido?"

"You were talking to José. That's where we're going."

I went over a few blocks and turned up an avenue wider than the main drag. There were tire ruts grooved coming and going on the side, like passing car tracks. The rest of the street was washboarded and chuckholed. I took it easy, the crankcase bumping the raised dirt between the wheel tracks at the deep spots.

All the streets away from town were unlighted. So the Zumbido ahead blazed up like a beach fire. The music carried from the bars as we rocked and bounced toward the lights.

I circled the long, three-block-square area that made up the settlement. The sidewalks were narrow and jammed with men. There were gangs of kids who'd come over the border. The few women you noticed walking alone probably figured to be hustlers.

I had to park a couple of blocks away. I worried about leaving the car, but the back streets were pretty busy. The hookers were standing behind the fences outside the little bungalows, the porches crowded with the studs that were waiting to go inside. Outside the crib shacks the tricks were standing in line smoking in the back yards.

This was the border town part, the vice trap, that was open all night. There was the section as you came in the gate: the souvenir places and stores that were closed now, and the few cafés; then the houses of the people; and then this Zumbido. But the gate was where they drew the line. You had to make your funny scenes in Mexico.

We pushed our way into this Manuel's Bar. It was lit up inside like a fight ring. It was a small place but loaded, I handed our way through to the long bar. Two bartenders were working. I ordered mescal for Lona and a bottle of Tecate beer. The bartender had dark glasses and looked like a character. He put the mescal bottle with the dead worm inside on the bar, watching. But Lona knew it. She poured herself another shot. Plenty of grasshoppers and big millers were drawn inside by the lights. The floor was slippery in places from the mashed ones. It was a standing bar, but someone brought two stools for us.

A girl was sitting on a small raised platform on top of the bar, before it turned to the wall. Her dress wasn't tucked under her. She was leaning over talking to two Mexicans below her. Drinking there, they had it pretty good for themselves. About a dozen girls were standing in the corner by the jukebox. There were booths along the wall behind us, with some girls and Americans and a few Mexicans in them. A couple would get up and go through the doorway at the end of the bar where the girl was perched. It happened regularly as I watched, the booths keeping turning over. If there was no drink coming, the girls by the jukebox would go straight through the doorway with whoever picked them out of the group over there. When they came out the girl would go back by the juke or hang around the bar. The guy either stopped for a drink or went out through the crowd at the door.

It was a trick bar, with the cribs out in back. Some of the girls were looking at us and making cracks to themselves.

"Let's split," I said to Lona, "we're in the wrong place." The juke was turned up full and the overall noise made you shout.

"Don't be self-conscious."

"They're not talking about me."

"The hell with them."

Some mariachis came in. I saw one of the girls point to us, and the four of them came over. They began playing and singing. I gave the head one a quarter and told him to go away. But they wouldn't. Some people were beginning to notice. The whore on the platform was grinning. She was a different one, sitting facing down the bar. She got down and went through the doorway with a kid who was pretty scared-looking. Another one was helped up to the seat. It was like where you came in, all right.

I didn't think you could get tired of looking. But I told Lona even bringing the stools for us was a form of insult, if you thought about it. She got up and stood, then. Then, finally, she couldn't stand the lousy mariachis, and they weren't going to leave, so we went out.

I drove back toward town. A block before the main drag I stopped in front of the Cortez Hotel. A car watchman was on duty outside. He wore an army shirt and pants and had a .45 on his belt. I gave him half a dollar to sit in the car. The hotel was on the second floor, built out over a shade arch, with stores and a café downstairs that were closed. We went up the flight of stairs. I rang the bell by a little glass-windowed office. A Japanese woman in a housecoat came out of the next door. She went into the office and pushed a pad through the opening in the glass. The room was two dollars.

The window looked out on the small park across the street. The lights of the Zumbido were off in the distance. I looked down at my car below.

I asked Lona what she wanted to drink that wasn't tequila and we still needed some papers. You can roll the tobacco out of cigarettes and poke grass into the tube, like José had meant but it doesn't pack right that way. I took the car out again. But the liquor stores on the drag were closed. I drove to the *abarrotes* next to the El Charro. I bought a bottle of Madero bourbon, two packs of papers, and two quarts of Cardinal beer.

When I came back, Lona had got the Japanese woman to give her a box lid. She had the grass cleaned from the seeds and twigs, scraping the leaves into a corner of the lid with a match book. I made two cigarettes with the papers.

I opened one of the bottles of Cardinal and the Madero and made a boilermaker. I filled the sink in the head to cool the other quart of beer. I had to wash out the glass because I'd forgotten to pick up a couple. We sat on the bed and passed the glass and joint Lona had going.

"They must have hurry-cured this jive in a stove," I said.

"No, it's strong pod. It can stretch you."

"Right now," I said. I was feeling the tingle in my scalp already.

"I wish we had some music."

Down the hall a radio was playing the mariachi stuff. People were going and coming down there.

"We wouldn't have to listen to that alley-cat yelling. The Yuma station has a cool deejay."

I got off the bed and put my shoes on. I went up the hall and knocked on the Japanese woman's door. She gave me her radio and she was listening to it. She was going to bed, she said. She wouldn't take any money from me.

There weren't any wall outlets in the room. I lifted the chair on top of the bureau. I got up and put the radio on the seat and connected it to the ceiling bulb outlet. Then we had the Yuma deejay.

"Don't let's fall asleep, Nicky."

"We won't."

"One-way Nicky. But that's cool, baby. You know I couldn't go through that ride again."

"If there's traffic on that road Saturday, I don't know."

"Some Mexicans with special visas come across."

"We might all make the joint."

"Don't even say it. What have Sand-o and Graemie been saying?"

"Nothing new."

"Anybody in jail I know this week?"

"They're either in or out."

"That's the truth almost."

"Sand-o was doing upholstering, I tell you? I think Graemie's been pushing some white stuff a little. Maybe not. You never know how he eats."

"Graemie the great white doughnut hunter."

"That's him."

"Give us a drag."

I handed her the roach. She dragged on it and gave it back. I shut one eye and watched hardly any smoke come when I exhaled slowly. She had one of the pillows propped against the knife-scarred headboard, and her legs across mine. She'd taken off her slip. It looked like mosquito netting, spread out on the bed. I leaned on my elbow, holding the glass. A little breeze was coming in the window and we had a drink, a smoke, and a radio all going. I was feeling good and I wasn't thinking about Saturday.

FOURTEEN

"You know, Nicky, I got the feeling everything is going right past me, that I've had it. Well, I've had it, all right. But what has happened to all of us, Nicky?"

Lona got spooky-talking when she was high. She came on real low and slow, and you had to strain some to hear her. I grinned at her.

"Nothing," I said. "We've done nothing, that's all. I've walked and talked big, myself, and been small change. I figured I could always park cars, or fix them on a gyp lot. Or run errands for connections. Hell, or even hustle pill pool. Until something good came along. Well, I was right I could keep doing that as long as I wanted."

"None of the bunch have done anything for the last seven years except go to jail. You went to Korea—"

"Not on purpose."

"Well, you weren't alone. I mean, though, since we left school. All this talk about teenagers now. Nobody paid attention to us."

"What did you want them to do?"

She held the roach, looking at it the way when you're not seeing anything. "Maybe they did. I don't recall. Give us drink."

She held the glass and roach out to me then, sitting up. "Take one."

I took them both.

"That's your trouble, old Nicky-o."

"Go pass your leaflets. Beat a drum."

"Not for you. Light us the other joint, will you?"

I got off the bed. I put the dead roach on the bureau.

I wet my finger and thumbed two papers. I pinched the grass into the fold of both, then put the bigger one aside and built a thinner one instead. I licked the ends and twisted the fire end tighter, then mouthed the joint wet to burn it slow. I lit the fire twist, pointing the joint down. The flame ran up blue. I held the joint straight and it went out. The grass was caught and I blew it up, air-dragging, and gave it to Lona.

I went up and looked out the window. I listened to the dogs barking. You could hear them off a long way. Across in the park the grasshoppers were going like steam whistles.

Sometimes it's the jive. You're good a minute ago, and now I could feel a bum kick coming on. Green grass will do that, or the seeds headache you. But this was all right pod.

I pulled off my shirt and tossed it at the bed. Lona smoothed it on the blanket. I reached the bottle of Cardinal off the bureau, swigged it, and put it back. I put my foot on the windowsill.

Lona came next to me. She took my arm and put it around her. "Tom kick, Nicky?"

I shrugged. "Or something."

"I know them. Talk it away. Oh, I wish I could split from everything. For good. Go off somewhere and try the whole scene over again."

"Maybe he intends to do you the favor. I was thinking about that. I'm probably dead wrong."

"I wish he would. He's not happy, himself."

"How often do you make it over here?"

"Every couple of weeks, sometimes. It's a thing I have to do, get off, get a change. He probably knows every time I've come over. He just has to look in my purse."

The moon was dead south now. There were two stars strung away a little behind it. Lona held the joint up for me. Someone was riffing on a sax on the radio. It sounded like the Laurindo Almeida album I knew. The radio there on top of the chair on the bureau was a crazy arrangement, all right.

I said, "I went along with this deal because I saw a way out. Of something. I wanted to talk to you about it. When I couldn't get you I saw I couldn't talk over the phone anyway. But the last few days I've been in and out of it. I've been pretty undecided."

"That's the story of your life, Nicky."

"Is it?"

"You never knew what you wanted. So here you are."

"There you are."

"If somebody told you you might be robbing a bank some day—"

"Look at what you're in."

She took my arm away, holding my hand. "But I tried to get out. No matter what you think my reason was."

"All of a sudden."

"That's how I was feeling. I wasn't going to hang around town any longer. What was there? I once had you, and then we didn't have anything. Because neither of us tried to keep it going. So when you were arrested, that was it. I didn't want you back. It would have been the same thing over again, those old beefs. Right then it seemed as if I'd been beefing all my life. What did I ever have at home but hassling, either?"

"You had that," I said.

"A lush of a father who would yell at me for smoking jive. *Him* talk to *me*. Sometimes I would forget, about him if I was lushed or loaded. I'd come in after school, and he'd be sitting in his chair, looking out the window with his bottle of red wine. I'd go over and kiss him, although I once swore I never would again. He'd push me away. He'd say, 'Drunk and smoking jive again,' and look out the window. And I'd real bad-mouth him, because I wanted to hurt him back. I'd say, 'Jive and lush don't use together, you mother. You know that.' He'd look up at me with that dago murder in his eyes. Then I'd laugh and walk out."

"You two used to go around."

"Oh, he would remember all my little tricks. *Mine*, yes. You know when he wouldn't let me out at night—just go to school and come home—how I would get the stuff off the kids anyway? And sit in my room smoking and fanning the air with a newspaper. Then come to supper so loaded I couldn't see the plate. And my skirt still smelling from the spark holes. But I'd stare him down. He was always staring, even not consciously, with that eye paralyzed from his stroke. He would call me a tramp and Mom would go in the bedroom. Then he'd go dragging his leg in there and shout at her if she was crying. But if I was loaded enough I wouldn't hear them. Once I sang real loud while he was cursing her and he stopped to listen. Then I had to run for the bathroom and I was sick and crying myself, into the john. That's why I moved out, and in with everyone. Anything to get out of there."

"It wasn't just anything."

"But so many things have gone wrong on me, Nicky. And now I'm twenty-six, and wondering if maybe it's too late to find something."

I held up my finger, steady.

"Go away. Two, there. Yes, I'm loaded now. I haven't

saved you butts either. We haven't got a roach holder." She tossed the cocktail out the window. "Light that big goodie. We'll be somebodies. You're a bank robber, and I'll be queen of the whores."

"I'm not one, yet. And you never were that."

"I've swung that way, Nicky."

"Because of me, not working. And not really that real way."

"How does this girl get the money to come over here and drink and get high?"

"You con that José. Or anyone."

"Why were the girls in Manuel's Bar giving us a bad time? Because I'm an outsider, not one of them. They know José. He's on the highway department. That's a character saying down here. It means a stud who hustles anything."

"He said he liked it out of jail."

"He's careful about grass. Or the hard stuff. He fixes me up with friends; you know? This is a tough town for a girl to come across to to swing, baby. You have to have the connections."

"You're pretty loaded, I think."

"I don't deny it. See that wallpaper move, yourself?"

"That's painted."

"You're no fun at all."

I lit the other joint. The Cardinal was warm now and tasted flat. We weren't drinking the boilermaker I'd made. I got the quart out of the filled sink in the bathroom, and took the cap off on the opener screwed to the door. A scorpion ran across the floor. I went to step on it and remembered my shoes were off. I set the bottle in the sink and got my shoe and found the scorpion in the corner and hit it. It was two inches long, with the stinger up waving. I had to hit it a couple of times before it cracked on the cement floor. The damn thing was nothing but a baby lobster.

I stood up. I looked at myself in the sink mirror and started laughing. That was pod, too. You could laugh or bawl. You could go either way and break up. I picked up the bottle, then couldn't hold it. I let it go back in the sink, it flopping over, the beer yellowing the water. I held on to the sink, lifting on it, but I couldn't stop laughing. I could hear the radio down the hall, louder through the wall now, and it was *Cielito Lindo* playing. I remembered Mrs. Flores used to put it on the changer, listening to all those songs, trying to pick up on Spanish. She could sing Spick after a while, but she couldn't talk it. But I'd picked it up running with the Mexican kids, who always had plenty of grass. Fat Mrs. Flores, who was Greek, and two hundred pounds. Who was married three times before little Flores. She'd balled like she invented it, she told you. Before Flores. Because that little Flowers was it. And she was a good damn big wife to him. Then he'd died.

"Nicky, no more for you."

"Remember Mrs. Flores?"

"She had a mustache. Now, *come out of there*. You'll total yourself."

I sat on the bed and tried to hold it back. I pushed back and leaned against the wall, rolled my head against the wall, banging it, and somebody knocked on the other side, yelling in Spanish. I swung over, choking, yanking the bedclothes up under me, balling them, and came off the bed in a straightening jump. I got off the floor, going toward the window with the bedding, and Lona grabbed my arm and whacked me in the face. She hit me across the eyes accidentally, and I dropped the stuff and leaned back against the bureau.

Lona had the joint, holding it for me. My eyes watered, stinging.

"Now *drag. Deep. Don't breathe.*"

I held my head down and felt the pod go in and spread out, then the poke there's like a small explosion. The lower part of my face pulled down, around my mouth and nose, and I licked my lips.

There was just the bare mattress, and I went back on it against the wall. I still had that action trying to get going in me, but fought against it. I breathed heavy, out loud. Lona got on the bed and sat cross-legged, pulling her dress across her knees. She was trying not to laugh.

"Remember when Mitch went real ape on just beers?" she said. "He wanted to clean out the Goodnight. On four beers."

"Lon wiped him out. I can still hear him tapping him."

"I had to smack you."

"It didn't feel like much."

"The way you were."

"Let's see, now."

I pulled her forward and, turning her, held her across me. I could smell her powder; she still used the same kind. It was called Cotillion. I didn't let her go until her breath came as hard as mine.

"I wish we could go away together, Nicky."

"So do I."

"You wouldn't want me, for good."

I ran my tongue over my lip. I had bitten it before. Something kept ticing in my face.

"Truthfully," she said.

"I think when I saw you there never was anyone

else for me," I said. "You remember back then. I knew it could be that way, but I wouldn't let it. Because I never could figure you out. I couldn't be sure how you felt, or if you would stay with me. So I turned, I guess, so I wouldn't get hit hard. Then I got it twice as bad. But I love you, Lona. You know it. You don't know how much, I don't think."

"If you had ever told me, just that way, I couldn't have left you, I would have stayed. And when I think how badly I've acted, how cold I've been."

"You're wrong," I said, "there."

She sat up. "Listen to me. No, listen. Yes, I'm easily aroused. But you know what has to come before that. I need to be high, half the time out of my mind, to do anything. *Yes*. Or it's no good. Because I feel sick to make it. I keep telling myself the next time will be another thing. But it isn't. Then I start looking again, to find someone else. That's how it's always been. You know what it's made me."

"I don't know anything."

"I've been coming over here for almost a year now, Nicky. That's the truth. I never gave him a real chance to forget."

"I don't give a damn. I'm not him."

"And I want you, again. So real God much. But I'm afraid of us. I'm afraid of myself."

"We can take it one thing at a time. We'd go easy. It would depend on me. We'd make out this time."

"I've got to clear my mind. I have to stop going back. But I don't know how not to."

"Leave it to me."

"You know my father is a lush, and didn't like you. But he never liked anybody I had over. He was jealous of me. I've never told anyone why.

"When I was ten he started coming into my room. It's the first time I'll never forget. Him getting onto the bed with me and holding me and I thought it was just the goodnight kiss. Then he got under the covers with me. And saying, 'Don't be scared, I'm not doing anything. But don't tell your mother, ever. Don't say a word or she'll be real mad at me.' Saying it over and over, and I didn't know what he was doing. I didn't know what to make of any of it. And two and three times a week after that. When I think of it now I get sick. I get crawly all over. But then I just didn't know what it was. Once Mom went back to Cleveland, when her sister died. The day we were to pick her up at the airport he drove into this back road, with a bunch of trees around. Then I began to feel something was wrong. You know how? Because it was daylight, and out there. And always before it had been in my room, and at night. I broke out of the car and he ran after me. He caught me and quieted me and made me get back in the car. We met Mom and she could tell something had happened. But I told her I wasn't feeling well."

I didn't say anything. I let her talk. She moved up and leaned back against me. She pressed my hand to the side of her face. When I first knew her, she'd held my hand like that in a movie, till my arm went numb across the back of the seat. But I didn't move it. I could still think of her holding my hand like that.

"I was pregnant when I was fourteen. He gave me three hundred dollars and told me to wait on the corner for a Chrysler. A man and woman picked me up and took me to an office in an apartment somewhere. I had a shot before I saw what the doctor looked like. After I got home I started to hemorrhage.

I called to Dad and he came in and said he would take care of it. A half-hour later he came in again, drunk, and said he couldn't reach the doctor. I got hysterical then, and Mom came in, but he sent her out. Finally he took me in the car to Harbor. He told me not to tell them anything, keep my mouth shut. I had the transfusion record, I think. They asked me who the doctor was, but I didn't know his name, anyhow. The hospital thought I was one more kid who had loused up her parents. That's what he told Mom, too. When he came to get me they sir'd him all over the place. He put on a real cool martyr look. And only I knew what he was. But that was the end. He never came near me after that. I would have had him arrested if he had. Even when I tried to forgive him, because he was sick or crazy, he would turn on me. Because he couldn't stand me around having that on him."

"He'll total himself drinking. Somebody said he had another stroke, I heard."

"Mom wrote me about it. I didn't answer."

"It's funny your mother never caught on."

"How could anyone be so stupid? Maybe my mom is. Or she suspected something but couldn't believe it. She's just a poor little ignorant Irish woman from Cleveland, married to a damn dago grocery clerk. I'm proud of the Italian in me but not of him, you bet. I just don't consider I've ever had a father. But I can't wipe his tom memory out of my mind. Well, my kids won't ever have him for any grandfather."

"You have Sand-o to thank, there," I said. "His damn weight-pressing."

"That, yes. But when I think of all the things I did, in the back seats of jalopies. And even helped push them afterwards. What a fish I was, Nicky. What a reputation I built up. But I didn't care. When you got me, Nicky, I'd been around some. But I saw something in you the others didn't have. Because you looked at me different from them. You were better than me, and the rest of them. You could think right, and you had a good sharp mind. So I wanted you to be someone, so I could have a man to look up to. You can't keep looking down on them, and yet wanting one so much as I do. I wanted to be a clean, real lady, because I was feeling dirty ever since I was a kid. But it didn't come true, even with you. Then it was Dave, because I thought the difference in ages. But I was wrong. So when he changed, and the balling I had done got written all over him, I used it as an excuse to do more. He wanted both of us to see a psychiatrist in L. A. once, but I told him to go in himself. Because the only way I could stand staying with him then was to come over here when I needed it. You know, now, how much that's been."

"Will you leave him when I get in touch with you?"

"I can tell him I want a divorce. I hate to, but I want to. Oh God, Nicky, if you really want me again. I'm so loused up. So mixed up. You don't know."

"Better wait until we make the play."

"I wish you weren't going through with it. It's a lousy idea, anyway. That ride, and all the rest of it."

"I'm thinking about the money."

"Because of me?"

"No. Where could I make that kind of money?"

"And never stop running. That's not my idea of starting over. It would be beginning at the end. He's out of his mind. I don't care what his reason is. He probably blames me."

"What for?"

"He can. Oh, Nicky—it's not a big one—it isn't. I'm not really hooked."

"We'd still need money."

"I guess we would. Some."

"Well, you have to be realistic. I mean about everything."

"Whatever you say."

"I couldn't back out if I wanted now. Besides, I don't."

"All right, Nicky."

I got off the bed and went to the bureau. I rolled a joint, a big one. I wanted to be straighter than I was. Lona walked over to the window, in the mirror. She moved lightly, always that nice to watch: so damn good-looking always: cool-looking, high-cheekboned, black-eyed and proud-looking. Sometimes I'd look at her, like now, and feel as if I was being sneaking about something. Then something would go *Jesus Christ* inside me quick. I lit the joint, my hand shaking in the mirror.

I sat on the edge of the bed and Lona came next to me. She took the joint and inhaled on it, long-dragging, shutting her eyes. The mirror on the bureau, slanting downward, reflected us. I got up and pulled the light string on the octopus. The radio went off.

"See what you did."

"I was getting that Edison."

"I want it on. You know."

I tugged the cord and the music came on. "Not always," I said.

"Now he remembers." She lay back on the uncovered mattress and put her hand out. "You just hot trot over here. Leave my little Japanese woman's radio be."

I went over.

"There. Look." I looked in the mirror, between the chair's legs. "Now you have two of me."

"I can see."

She turned away in the mirror. "Sir. What are you doing to me?"

"Which one is that?"

"Both us, man. Boy."

"Damn you, Lona," I said, under my breath. It had been coming on.

"Now, *hey*. What's *that* for?"

"I love you," I said. "I think it says here I'm going to crack up."

"That's so wonderful to hear, baby. But don't again like that, baby. Tell yourself not to."

"No. Not like before." I slapped myself hard on the back of the neck.

"Oh, Nicky—baby—I'm sorry—damn *me*. Oh here I go."

We held each other's hands tight and I looked in the mirror once underneath the chair. It was funny how you sometimes looked silly when you felt just the opposite.

"*Hey*," I said, "easy."

"You started it. Oh, Nicky, I love, love, love you. I am so ever *hung* on you. I could eat the word."

"I could something like now."

"What*ever* are you trying to do now forever?"

"Just wait. Ten minutes and the world's over."

"It better not be." She was laughing. "Now, honestly, tell me what you're doing."

"Mirrors don't lie."

"I like to hear it. You know."

"What don't you want?"

"You're so really right."

I said it. "Now listen to the music."

"Let them go play up the river. You don't know how that affects me. I want to see, hear, everything. All-at-once."

"You'll do to watch out for trains."

"You whistle for the crossing, anyway."

"That's been done."

"Who isn't bragging? Oh, someone is *pretty* good all right. Nicky, Nicky— Oh I want you to hurt me, I *do, hurt* me—"

I was going to tell her. I was going to hold her down now and almost shout it at her. That all the liquor and grass she could use was no help. Nor the hard stuff she was back on. Because I'd felt those marks on her arms the first time I came out. And I knew he'd be wanting to get rid of her. And it was why I'd come back. So there had to be a Saturday. Because I would go to hell with him for her. And, maybe, later.

But, instead, I reached the roach off the bureau, and dragged, until my head started going faster. So when I lay up along beside her and held her against me, feeling her everywhere all over, inside me, I didn't care about anything.

And when it came, and she said the one or two things about her father, it was nothing. It was always over that quickly. And using that word, you could think it was you.

But she hadn't remembered I knew.

FIFTEEN

I woke up with a mouth tasting like I'd been eating old newspapers, and my head had a weight rolling inside it. I was wiped all right. I thought of all the don'ts there were, and included sleep. It should have been the first. It was dark outside, but I was afraid to look at my watch. Then I did. But, somehow, it was only five-fifteen.

I went up to the window. A morning mist was lifting, blowing cold on me. The sill was wet and I stood shaking like I didn't know better, looking out. The lights of the Zumbido were still burning off there, but fading now in the grayness. Below, some peddlers were crossing to the park, carrying tables on their heads. To set up their outside markets, I guessed. I went over and woke Lona up.

The shower was plugged so you had to shut it off when it rose to the drain curbing. I dressed, then, while Lona went in. I disconnected the radio, took it up and left it inside the office. When we came down to the car I woke the watchman. He leaned against a Chevvy's fender, still yawning, while I warmed up the engine.

Lona and I had the headaches and that burned-out pod taste in the mouth, and there wasn't time enough left for breakfast. But we were still lucky on the time. I could have slept right through.

The radio came on with the ignition, with some early bird's program across the line. I switched him off.

"You don't think they'll want to look," I said again to Lona.

"I'm not *sure*. But they don't unless they've been tipped. Nicky, I've been across before."

That was still a sore spot, I thought. I wanted to forget it. I wished, now, she hadn't told me.

"If you don't relax a little. You should see your mouth, Nicky, so tight. This is you." She showed me.

Lona had the grass rolls flattened inside her bra. But there wasn't any problem about the guns, either. There wouldn't be any because there couldn't be. Because I hadn't thought about them, at all, until we were across. And then it was too late.

Now, driving down the main drag, and seeing the gate there ahead, I slowed down. "I hope this goes right," I said, mainly to myself. I was sweating inwardly.

"We're in. We're as good as across. This fat old inspector is cool. He doesn't give a doodledydamn."

"I'd like it if he was blind pig."

He was sitting on a folding chair on the raised walk alongside the driveway. He got up as I coasted up, fat and sloppy in his uniform without a tie. He had steel-rimmed glasses that reflected the light. He glanced at the back seat once, then looked down at me. The Mexican Customs wasn't around.

"Where were you born?"

"Denver," I said. Lona told him California.

"What are you taking from Mexico?"

"Nothing," I said.

"Nothing," he said, nodding. He ducked out of the window. I looked up at him. He was looking across the roof of the car.

He looked down at me. "Will you open your trunk, please?"

I'll tell you something. Maybe, nothing. Those guns

were Sand-o's all right. But we would be held until that was checked out. Don't think there wasn't going to be some hot questioning, either, about all those pieces, and the shells. Madrid would be called, too, because of Lona's identity. And there no doubt was some law about bringing firearms into Mexico, too; especially undeclared.

Well, the bank was out. I saw it go. And everything else with it. Because I had thought of nothing but that speed run over. And I couldn't try to run for it now. They would radio ahead my license number.

I pulled the keys from the ignition and got out. Walking back I looked at the sky, low and flat, and stretching wide and far, clear blue with the sun just coming up. It was nice, I guessed. But I wanted to be sick.

I unlocked the trunk. I released the catch, it snapping loose, and wondered what I was going to say. I let the lid go up.

I heard my breath drawing in. The guns weren't there.

"Step back, please."

I moved back. I couldn't think.

He leaned into the trunk and felt around the spare well. He got inside, kneeling, feeling the space behind the back-seat partition. I couldn't see Lona, the raised lid cutting her off.

He backed out and pulled out the mat. I even helped him putting it back. He didn't say a thing, and I couldn't. Then he went up and asked Lona to step out. I helped him take the back seat forward, then the rug up; then the front and the mat. I took the stuff out of the glove compartment, then lifted the hood when he asked me. While he looked around the engine

Lona, standing on the other side, motioned to me. I didn't go over. A car went across in the next lane, waved over. The people in it big-eyed us.

He let down the hood and I thought, it's the hub-spinners, or even the door panels next. But he was through for himself. He told me I could go, and sat down in his chair, folding his arms. He didn't look at us as I drove out. He was a pretty cool inspector. Yes. Sure.

"Will you stop hitting the wheel?"

"I can't," I said.

"Well, you wouldn't rather he'd found them?"

"*No*. But I don't know what to *think*."

"Then don't. You know what I do? They weren't in the trunk. That's a woman's intuition."

"I know they were."

"When did you look? The last time."

"Checking in the motel. They stayed in the car."

"They were taken out around the Zumbido, then."

"Sure. Except the trunk was *locked*. I opened it."

"Someone used a skeleton key."

"They use a jimmy."

"All right, jimmy. But was *he* disappointed he didn't find his old bundle of hay."

"The store next to the café. That was the place. Where I bought the papers. José said not to. It's lucky that inspector didn't put a matron on you."

"We were turned in for spite. Somebody did it for meanness. They said we had a big bunch of grass. That's what he was looking for."

"Those bastards. Oh, Jesus," I said, then, "what about the guns?"

"I thought you weren't going to use them under any circumstances."

"We needed the ones we have to show. You have to have those."

"Well, I'm glad. In a way."

"You are?" I said.

"Well, no. Can't you buy them?"

"It's trouble. Besides the money. Do you know what that collection cost?"

"Nicky, I'm sorry. But I can't get excited. I feel badly about them, for your sake. But it was a whole lot better than having them found."

"They were my responsibility. I don't know what to do."

"Just drive a little faster. A little. We've got to hurry now."

The sun was up already bright and hot. I drove sweating and I couldn't think from the night and hardly any sleep and nothing to eat didn't help.

SIXTEEN

I opened the door and the two of them were waiting for me. I saw the cigarette butts in the ashtray on the table between the beds.

"Hello, lover," Sand-o said to me.

I closed the door and sat down in the chair by the window. I could hear a kid crying in the next cabin.

"Clue us in, lover," Sand-o kept it up. "How was the action?"

I shook out a cigarette.

"Don't needle me," I told him. I leaned forward. I was tired and nervous. I felt like to jump.

I looked at Graemie, the sheet up under his chin. His feet were uncovered, sticking over the edge of the bed. He looked like some long white-faced stiff. He hadn't said anything to me.

Then I said, "Somebody took the pieces from the trunk."

"They *what?*" Sand-o said.

Graemie didn't move. He kept looking at the ceiling.

"Where were you?" Sand-o said to me.

"Mexico."

"Oh, *yeah?* How come?" And then, as if remembering, "*What* about the pieces?"

You can go over something too much, rehearsing what you're going to say. And it goes flat coming out, not right-sounding. Sand-o would be blowing his top, yelling. He would be all over me.

I felt the tightness go out of me. Lona might have hit it. I was thinking, now. They were a lot of guns.

I went to the closet and pulled open the door. I could

see the Winchester's case sticking out below my topcoat. I didn't look further in there.

I turned around and shot my cigarette at Sand-o. He was leaning on his runt arm. He slapped the butt back at me. I stepped on it on the floor. I stood by the foot of the bed, studying him.

"I knew you'd ball with her. You couldn't stay away. You can't take care of yourself, you knocked-out character."

"Don't call me a knocked-out character."

"Did you want to show them to her? Play little big boy with guns?"

"Why didn't you say you sneaked them out?"

"When you were in the joint up front, with Graemie. When I asked you for the keys to get the pod, that's when. I don't like to have my property running around the country—or out of it. Cop out, how's the shacktown down there?"

"I'm getting sicker of you."

"Who do you love?"

"You heard me."

"I'll never tell. I don't have to. He knows."

"He knows crut."

"He called after you left. And don't call *me* a sneak; that was Lona the first time, wasn't it? He gave your phony name and I answered it. He saw the car gone."

"What did you say?"

"I told him you took a ride out to the desert, this trap was bugging you. I said maybe you went on to Yuma. Did I do right?"

"What did it cost you?"

"It made a liar out of me."

"That's worth nothing."

"I could cut my throat."

"That would be worth something."

"He took off to run you down. After he told you not to take your jalopy on the road, he said. He was frosted good."

"I'll story him."

"You don't have to. The deal's knocked, anyway."

"Get out of here," I said to him.

He reached over the side of the bed and picked up the newspaper on the floor. He skimmed it at me. I caught it as it fanned out.

"Right in there is the biggest break you're getting in your life. On the second page. I don't care how long you goof, that's all the gravy you've got coming."

It was the local paper, skinny like a throwaway. I folded it to the second page. He had a news item boxed out in pencil:

WAREHOUSE BURGLAR
CAUGHT IN BRAWLEY

Jaime de la O, a Mexican national, was chased and apprehended early yesterday by Brawley police while driving away from a hardware store it was alleged he had burglarized. Brawley police said de la O, 25, used a hacksaw last night to cut the padlock off the back door of the Superior Hardware Company. Waffle irons, toasters and other appliances, along with a collection of power tools and small motors, were found in de la O's car.

In further questioning, de la O, who entered the country illegally two months ago, reportedly admitted several similar burglaries in the Valley. One, notably, was the Davidson's Discount Stores warehouse burglary in Cuesta last July 21st. Some of the large haul of merchandise taken from

Davidson's warehouse was recovered in de la O's room in El Centro.

"I picked that sheet off the stand outside the joint up front. I ran out of beer when you cut out. I couldn't make this TV go, so I took that to read. I read everything in it before that hit me. Then I went back and read it six times."

"Was that enough?" I asked him.

He didn't know about Davidson's, the write-up Lona had seen on the job when it happened. It was just guessing, anyhow, that Madrid had taken the place. So, now, he hadn't. It had just been a coincidence. And it didn't make any difference either way.

"I've been laying here thinking all night. While you weren't around."

"About this thing?"

"The stuff you fenced off for him. That wasn't him."

I looked at the paper again, and laughed. "Who was it? This de la O?"

"I said you were a dummy. Who said the whole scam play stunk? But would you buy it? Hell, no. Because you're a knocked-out character."

"Listen," I said to him.

"So he was down on his gig, yeah? They wouldn't up him to sergeant, or some deal, so he was going to show them. So he knocks over some local joint and gets you to peddle the stuff. That goes good, so he gets to studying about the bank here. You know him and he knows you. You figure he's a real goofing fuzz because he balled with that knocked-out Lona, then married her. He knows that's how you make him. So he cuts you in on a buck, and gets you to forget, even, he busted you. He can't come out with this scam bank deal right away, though, because it's too much. So he works you up more with the fencing gimmick. Then he comes on with the bank spiel. He lets you off the hook the time you were out here because he's getting what he wants, too. Anyway, he doesn't give a damn. He's got you by the gonicles, so he's become your favorite character. You're an honest-to-God believer in him. Give me some nicotine, Graemie."

Graemie had his head in a cloud of smoke. His knees, raised, made a tent of the sheet. He tossed over the pack of cigarettes.

I sat at the end of the bed Sand-o was in. I put down the paper. He moved his cigarette at me. He was red-faced, his eyes opening and closing when he got hot.

"It takes three to rob a bank, he says. So that puts me and Graemie in his barrel. Then you almost goofed the whole bit for him when you got your jalopy reported out here. That's how come I took the pieces last night. For insurance against more of your screw-ups."

"Keep going," I told him.

"But we're supposed to need a beast for that run, or any getaway; so he still has to use yours. But why as is? Why wouldn't he have you paint it at Scheib's for twenty-three skins? Graemie, on the way to the big scene Saturday. *Why?* Because he *has* to take that chance. He knows your car from the old days, when he busted you. And that's part of the deal—him making your jalopy when the time comes. Brother, I can still hear that crack of his up in your pad: 'I got a deal tailor-made for you boys.'"

"Go on."

"We've all been brainwashed by the snow he's been shoveling. All right, me, too. That, and our own damn jerkiness. Hell, if we were caught in the action, he'd be twice as washed-up as us. And if we split clean away, he'd have the worry every day we'd be caught and cop out on him. We'd be around his neck from then on. Any time we copped out we could finger him good. We could prove we knew him and Lona. Louis saw him when he came in the place after you. My dad would spend dough to nail him with us, to salvage the good old family name some—what I've left him of it—because it wasn't our idea. Even George the fence would testify to nail a fuzz."

"Not George."

"Yes, George."

"That stuff was hot from somewhere. It was new."

"Will you *see* it? Wake up. I figure Madrid thought you might try to check on him. Or maybe he didn't. Anyway, he patterned that scam fencing off this Davidson's job a month ago. I'll make book on it. It might even have given him the whole idea. Only he went out and bought the stuff, on time, if he didn't have the loot. Then made you think he thieved it. But you didn't do any checking. You ran out here to goof, was all. If I hadn't seen that item in there—hell, you should kiss my heels, three joints up."

"Lona saw about that. The original story on the job. She takes the paper. She looked it up for me. She told me about it last night."

"Well, bring her around. I'll kiss hers."

"Later on that talk."

"I don't need it, you know." He got out of bed. He went to the closet and put his slacks on. "Me, with my arm—that bit—and that horse crut. *Man.*"

"What's he doing it for? What's the point?"

"What *point?*" He ran between the beds and grabbed

Graemie. "You *dig* him? Jesus, *dig* him!" He shoved Graemie over. He turned and put his foot on the bed, leaning toward me. He spit a piece of tobacco.

"This Saturday, you knocked-out character, you and me are going into his bank and sack it up, with Graemie out in the car. We'll come out on schedule, like he's figured for us, because we got that ride to make supposedly. Only, as we hit the street, there will be a light drawback. Because that armored truck will come up right then. With him playing Mary's little lamb in the fuzz car."

"What? What *for?*"

He rubbed his hand across his mouth. "Because he's a heat. He's never changed. Don't lose *everything else.* He took a bum rap for that damn Lona. But this is his career, his work—can I quote you? And he's out here at the end of the line; one good push and he's out of the country. Who the hell lives here but the melon- and cotton-pickers? Christ, he gets seventy-five a week, and it's a hundred in the shade. And they don't even like him. That's probably the one thing he hasn't scammed about. But he *sticks*. Because he's a *heat, all the time*, and he wants to square himself, and get back to god-damn civilization. He can go to plenty of towns in the state, no matter about his age, after the publicity he'll get breaking up a bank hold-up. He'll get himself a deal on any real-sized force that doesn't use civil service."

"You said we could bag him if we got caught."

He turned around and went to grab Graemie again. Graemie held him off.

"Oh, Christ. If all the Greeks were dumb as you, there'd never be restaurants."

"Spill it."

"You won't be around to *talk*. None of us will. It's going to be crossfire. We'll be hit by that World truck and him together. We'll be killed—murdered—goddamn you for getting us in this."

Graemie was looking at me, sitting up in the bed. "He's right, Nick."

"Hell," I said.

Sand-o said, "He's *got* to. There's no other scene for him. Otherwise, he'd never get away with it. Didn't I say it from the beginning?"

"You're overboard. He wouldn't."

"He killed that Sherry kid and the other one, robbing the Pig Burger, didn't he? He was off duty, too. He emptied his gun at them. They didn't fire once. And that was a lousy drive-in. This is a *bank*."

I shook my head. "I'm not with you. You're wrong, that's all."

"Why don't you wait and see then? Charge his bank. When he chops you with the riot piece they have in the car, come back and see me."

"Stop talking stupid. Suppose he did? What about Lona's testimony?"

"He'd say he came into town to ask you to stay away from her. That's his story. It's why he let himself be seen, like in Louis', and coming to Carroll's after you. But he holed up in your pad to meet Graemie and me, you noticed. Another thing, when you got your car reported, it proved to him she was keeping on chippying with you. That's how he'd use that."

"Why didn't he turn me in, if he knew it was me? I could have been picked up in town."

"His answer will be he suspected something more was happening, because you were carrying a gun. He once busted you for grass when you were shacking with her. So he figured maybe you were out here to make a connection over the border, through her, and bring some goodies across. That's just a guess. But he has some reason, you bet, like it."

"You have too many answers. For him."

"Don't give me Lona hasn't made a connection over there. *Her?* Tell me she wouldn't have."

"If I was running anything, would I wear a gun into a liquor store?"

"You did, didn't you?"

"I was lushed."

"Well? Who told you to be?"

I didn't answer him.

"So he kept quiet on you, and decided to wait. That's his line, later. If he was wrong, he could always have turned you in. It was no big deal, anyway. You didn't do anything but carry a piece. But if he found out you were bringing anything across he could have set a trap for you, with the department in on it then, and maybe break up a ring over there."

"You're giving him credit for a lot of big planning."

"What's bigger than what he intends doing?"

"According to you. You're reading everything into a little newspaper piece. You're just guessing all the way."

"Sure I am. Can I look inside his head? Just say I'm close."

"You want me to?"

"What the hell do I care? I *know* I'm right. I have to second-guess how he'll change his story to fit that rumble you got on yourself. The rest of it figures."

"You're getting ahead of yourself. You talk like the action's already happened."

"I just want to be one up on him. You'll never be. I'll

bet he's even got witnesses in Santa Lucia who saw you there with her last night. When he knew you were gone, I'll book the first thing he did was go in his house and look for her. Then called them at the border to watch if your car came across."

"I was stopped coming back. They searched the car. That's why I knew the guns were out."

"Good God, that's right. You would have had them with you. Christ, you almost sunk him right then. *Listen*, you know what I think *right now?* You getting stopped: I bet he's had the green light on this right from the start. I bet the department and the Customs were in on that trap. He took advantage of you going across, and set it up. Except only he knew it was a phony. And you almost killed everything for him by being caught with the pieces."

"Don't get carried away. I bought some grass and was turned in. But they didn't find it."

"Oh? Yeah? Where is it?"

"Lona has it."

"You know, I'm going to keep an eye on you. Somebody should. I'm not kidding."

"Who made those trips with me to Tijuana? When we brought things back?"

"Were we charging a bank the day after?"

"Would that have gotten us off, if we mentioned it?"

"Where was I? Christ, I'm getting dizzy."

"You've been doing too much figuring. You're all balled up."

"Hey," Graemie said. "It's raining."

He pointed his finger at Graemie. "Goddamn you, shut up."

It was though; now I could hear it. I went to the window and parted the blind slats. It was coming down with the sun shining. I saw the fat landlady go past, waddling ahead of a car, holding a newspaper over her head. She opened one of the cabins across the way.

"Look," Sand-o said to me. "The next time he sees you is when we come out of the bank. That's the one thing for sure, that always was. Right after he makes your jalopy outside. Later, they'll figure you got the idea for the play from Lona. When she copped out to you about the detail he'd be working on Saturday. And the more she tells the real story, if she even tries to, the worse it'll sound like lies, from her. It'll come out this is the second time she's dragged him down, after he was kicked off the force in town because of her. He'll shake her fast when it's all over."

"You think they won't listen to her?"

"You know damn well nobody would. She's a junkie, and she's dingie. You just never admitted it, or faced it."

"What do you mean?"

"I bet he's sick of making it with her and being called that 'Daddy Don't.' Hell, does she know she even says it? Sure, it's a gas for a while. But later on that noise pretty quick."

I went toward him.

"Hombre," Graemie said, "knock it off."

"You want to go? Come on, be nice to yourself."

"Take it back," I said.

"Make me."

"You gimp arm," I said. "You mother. Come on."

"I'm giving you three."

He laughed. "You playing red-light? O. K., I take it back. I don't feel like fighting, anyhow. I'm just burned up at myself."

I went in the bathroom and took off my shirt. I hung it on the doorknob.

"What gives?" He leaned against the door, the cigarette slanting in his mouth. His blond beard was still wiry, scraggly-looking. I looked at his yellow narrowed eyes against the cigarette smoke. I wondered what I ever saw in him.

"I'm cutting out."

"Where to?"

"I don't know."

I took my razor from the cabinet and injected a blade in it. I thought about shaving the way I felt.

"Wait a minute. You think I'm right about Madrid? Or has he been leveling with us?"

Graemie came to the door. He was so tall and skinny in his shorts it was pitiful. "It adds up, Nick," he said slowly, "It's a scam deal, I think."

He was straight a little, I saw now, close, his pupils contracted.

"How would you know?" Sand-o said to him.

"Maybe he does," I said. "More than you."

"Good. Just tell me I'm right on the double-cross. Throw all the rest out."

"Maybe," I said. I ran the water in the sink.

"Then listen some more."

"What's there left?"

He reached over and turned off the tap. "Come out of here!"

"For what? It's finished."

He put his face in front of me and grinned his broken nose at me.

"We're not through. We're still taking us a bank, old buddy."

SEVENTEEN

It rained the rest of the morning, but the motel cabins were filled by noon. People were coming into town early for the holiday weekend. Six years ago, they said on the coin radio, it snowed in a flash storm on the road to the sandhills. But it didn't stay down long; so if you hadn't seen it all even whiter out there you wouldn't believe it. I tried to picture it. Then, when we had our gear squared away, I rolled my car away from the door. Then we ran through the rain up to the café.

Some of the people who had checked in were inside eating. You saw the riding skirts breaking out already, with those shoestrings they wear around the collar. We stood at the bar waiting to sit down. Sand-o was wearing his trench coat. He opened it but kept it on. A party got up and we took their booth. The lighted beer sign in the window kept the glass from steaming up. The sun was gone in now and there were clouds black as oil smoke. The trucks going by on the highway were using their dims and trailer lights.

Madrid hadn't phoned all morning. After we ate, and were back in the cabin, we decided Sand-o would call him at the house by one-thirty. When he'd talked to Sand-o last night, Madrid said he would call after he came off duty. That would have been seven o'clock. We'd had it arranged to meet him at the Pass at two, to go in town with him. But he was going to call in the morning, anyway. But now he hadn't this late. And we were hung up.

Talking over how we'd really been taken by Madrid,

when it had once looked all right, we were afraid if we waited now we would get spooked, or maybe, even, chicken. Then we wouldn't go on anything. Graemie ran up to the café twice to get quart-size containers of coffee. I was getting loaded on that black joe, and Camel-high.

We had the easy way out more now. We didn't have to come out, as far as I was concerned, now; and we could go back. Except there was no sense to it.

Well, our town. It was a city, but pretty much a resort, too. People came to it to get a beach tan and healthy. There's Chamber of Commerce weather almost the year around. But every place has trains coming and going. And what we'd done in town were things we'd had so long that was it. There was nothing left of any real interest to us. I think Graemie, keeping quiet, maybe thought different. A character, a real wig, thinks to himself on plenty of things, the opposite of you. But I couldn't go back and have things the same, unchanging, again. Not getting away now and looking back. After these past few days.

I still didn't go along with Sand-o entirely. It's pretty hard seeing yourself getting killed in advance. But there was no argument against it. And we had it in hard for Madrid in another way; almost as bad. Because he had promised us something, then made us see it, and it never was there.

So at one-fifteen we were caught in the middle; afraid of us going, and that we wouldn't. And that was pretty pure frustration.

The fat landlady came to the door. There was a call for Ralph Williams, she said. Sand-o swung off the bed to take it for me. It was a woman, the landlady said. Then I didn't take my raincoat.

I ran up to the office.

"Nicky. Is he with you?"

"No. He isn't here."

"He hasn't come in. He hasn't called, either."

"Well—he hasn't called here," I said. The landlady was coming in the door. She sat down in the armchair behind the desk.

"Can't you talk there?"

"A little," I said.

"I called the station house. They said he left at the regular time. I thought he'd be with you."

"He was going to call."

"I feel funny. I feel as if something's happened."

"Well, you were right about the other stuff. You know? Sand-o had them."

"All the time?"

"Yes."

"Why couldn't he tell you?"

"His idea of joking."

"I feel funny, Nicky. I don't know why. I haven't been to sleep. I've been watching the rain out the window."

"You and everybody."

"I wish you could talk."

"Go ahead."

"Because, Nicky. When he comes in, I'm going to tell him."

I looked at the fat landlady. "We had that settled."

"I've been thinking a lot of things over, sitting here. It's almost like you and I are our last chance for each other, Nicky. Especially, you, for me."

"That's good, but—"

"Nicky, I can put it down. There's just that one scene. It's hard, but you can do it. You can help me."

"Yes. But wait on the other."

"Nicky, you won't do anything Saturday. It won't happen."

"No?" I said. "Why?"

"When I tell him I'm going to leave."

"That won't affect it."

"Nicky. He has his pride. He couldn't go on with you."

"He knows what he wants."

"It isn't me, anyway. So I'm going to tell him."

"A minute ago it was his pride."

"You said that wouldn't affect it, anyway."

"He's been shutting his eyes. Leave them that way."

"No."

"All right. And then what?"

"Isn't that up to you?"

"Yes. So I say wait."

"We won't need money if I put it down."

"Everybody likes to eat."

"Do they have to thieve to do it?"

"Maybe soon, with the cost of living."

"I was serious."

"No. Nor to turn *eis eis* on, either," I said. Fatso looked up at me, sniffing. She coughed.

"That hurt. If you meant it to."

"No," I said.

"Character talk. I haven't heard it in a long while."

"Long isn't enough."

"I'm still thinking of last night. We talked a storm up. So many things. Was I a little high?"

"A little."

"You were, too. But you were wonderful."

"You were."

"You Nicky. You, too. I mean the way a woman feels, though. I'd like for you to come over here. Can't you,

Nicky?"

"You know I can't."

"No, I don't." There was a pause. "I want to have it done and finished with, Nicky. What do you think this is doing to my conscience? Have you thought of that? I've forced myself not to. You don't even know what I'm talking about."

"Don't be that way."

"You can call me the next time. Nicky."

"I will. Just story him when he comes in. You went across there alone."

"Nicky. I love you."

"The same thing."

"Tell me."

"You know."

"Say it. I don't care who's listening there."

"When I call you."

"All right. Good-by, Nicky."

"Good-by," I said. I didn't want to say her name. I put down the receiver. Fatso sat back in her chair, grunting.

"Thanks," I said. For nothing.

"Are you people checking out?"

"I think so."

"I saw you loading over there."

"I think we're checking out."

"That's at two o'clock. Don't forget the key."

"If we go I'll bring it over."

I came back into the cabin.

"Well, he hasn't been home."

Sand-o got up from the bed. "It's stupid. Doesn't she know where the hell he is?"

"Fatso wants to know if we're checking out."

"I'll check her out."

He went to the door and opened it. The rain was noisy on my car's roof outside. A De Soto went by, its tires hissing in the gravel. Sand-o hooked the door closed with his boot. "It's almost two now."

"Five of."

"We'll go."

"He forgot to call. He's probably there waiting for us."

"If he isn't," Graemie said, "we'll lose the cabin."

"So we get another one, idiot. You like it here?"

"The television just stinks," Graemie said. "Like you."

"I haven't tried to adjust it, yet. Watch me."

The television was on a table with casters. He went over and swung it around. Before I knew it, he'd ripped the cardboard backing off the set. "What—" I said. He ran his hand around the inside, yanking, and brought out a few of the wires and resistors. "Sand-o fixes anything." He threw the things back inside and wedged the cardboard back so it stayed. He turned the set back to the wall.

"You crazy bastard," I said.

"It never worked right, did it?"

"It didn't cost anything."

"That was why. Don't stand there. You checking us out?"

"You're something," I said.

"Go make your errand, will you?"

I took my raincoat from the top of the closet door. I took the key off the bureau. I walked up to the office, feeling the .38 shells, loose, in the pocket of my raincoat.

EIGHTEEN

Sand-o had the engine running, the exhaust drifting back white in the rain. Graemie sat in the middle, slid down, hunched up. I got in beside him. Sand-o was an all-right one-armed driver, but there wasn't a spinner on the wheel for him. He took off the brake and we rolled down the little incline of gravel.

The out-of-towners were starting to kick it around in the café. They didn't have much else to do in the cabins. I saw the fat landlady standing inside the back screen door, the lights and the noise behind her. She watched us drive out, her hands on her hips, blurred in the rain on the window.

We hit the highway and Sand-o put the parking lights on. His beard and flattened nose made him look rugged, heavier trench-coated, his cigarette hanging from his mouth. Graemie had his rain hat pulled down low, his mouth a line in his long white face. None of us looked easy, I thought. We couldn't be.

When we came to Rialto Pass the windshield was clouding up. Sand-o turned on the blower. I gave him the red rag from the glove compartment after cleaning my side. A car swung toward us wide around on the curves and Sand-o put the headlights on.

We had the radio going on the news. The announcer said it was hailing in the northern Valley towns. It was unusual weather, you could take his word for it. Last year it hadn't rained a full inch in the region; anyone who wanted to buy any cats or dogs—I turned the station. We were passing the last road fork, with the group of railed mailboxes at the turn, with the rain falling darker now against the hillsides.

Sand-o drove past the fire trail to the next curve. No cars were coming and he passed twice backing around to come back. We came back down and parked on the shoulder.

We couldn't go up the fire trail. It was mud-heavy now. Sand-o turned off the lights and I got out. Graemie sat forward and I pushed the seat ahead and got in the back. I put my feet on the suitcase on the floor.

We sat, smoking, waiting for Madrid if he was coming. I looked at my watch. It was two-twenty. Now and then a car made the curve below, its headlights whitening the windshield. The wind wings were open but Sand-o kept wiping off the moisture.

Sand-o and Graemie were going in with him. That was what we had worked out. I was supposed to be hung over from my fling in Yuma, so I wouldn't be along. I would drive my car to the bank's parking lot, then, and meet Sand-o and Graemie inside. Graemie would go out to my car. Sand-o and I would take the bank while Madrid waited a block away. We would be in Mexico when he found out. He wouldn't talk. You don't drive thieves to a bank and wait for them. And we would be alive to involve him.

I wondered how long the rain would keep falling. It was a freak, but a break for us; what decided us to go all of a sudden. I could drive in it, she had good rubber. I could lay it down without traction-waving the treads any more on wet paving than dry. The heat slowed down in wet weather though. You saw that when they went by, just pushing the siren. The rain was a major thing, all right. It cut visibility. It meant less people and cars would be out, and we were wearing raincoats and hats. People always seemed to remember your clothes later. Now they couldn't tell about Sand-o's arm too carefully either. And it could stop raining any time.

I wondered how the parade and rodeo would be re-scheduled if it rained through Saturday. If it rained out the weekend it would be some Labor Day everywhere. Some people had come a long way, probably, for the celebration in town. Just being spectators at something was their idea of action. Well, we had a little something to do, more than watch. Because we had never done anything before.

Headlights rounded the curve ahead, then they slowed. I took my cigarette below the seat. I crouched down. When the lights came on Sand-o and Graemie their shadows stretched, jigsawing, on the headliner.

I heard an engine race, then gears grind. Sand-o blew the horn. He cursed and opened the door. He banged it shut and the car shook. He went up ahead yelling something.

"What's the matter?" I asked Graemie. He didn't get out and he should have.

"Stay down, hombre. There's Madrid."

But I looked over the back of the seat. I saw Madrid's Plymouth dipping into the water-filled gully alongside the shoulder. You couldn't see him inside with his windows vapored up.

He bucked his car, jumping the clutch, and the front end came up. The bumper slammed into the mud that had slid down from the top of the fire trail. Then he powered her, his wheels spinning water, grabbing in the gully, and he started going up. He skidded and grabbed and you could smell his clutch burning through the wind wing.

Sand-o was in front of us, not yelling now, watching him go up.

Madrid made the level where the burned-out house was. His taillights flipped up, leveling, and disappeared. You could see his headlight beams ahead, then, around the hill, cutting through the rain above the road. Then they went out. Sand-o stomped back to the car. He was blowing, raving.

I got back up on the seat.

"He *waved* at me!"

"Why didn't he stop?" I wasn't asking him the question.

"I'll tell you when I sound him! Graemie! Come on!"

"It's two-thirty," I looked at my watch.

"We have to get him off the goddamn hill! *Now!*"

"He'll make it down."

"Oh, you guaran*tee* it?" He twisted his mouth. "Like everything else?" He ran toward the beginning of the trail. Graemie got out, leaving the door swinging open, long-legging it after him.

I pulled it shut. Then I threw my legs across the seat and slid over behind the wheel. My raincoat bunched up behind me. It made a knot in my back. The hell with it. The hell with everything, now, I thought.

I watched Sand-o and Graemie go up the hill, jumping, stepping over the snake-cuts Madrid's wheels had made in the mud before he caught traction in the bordering weeds. I couldn't think why he'd kept going after seeing the car. I didn't know how he'd got up there, either. Sand-o was hustling, getting ahead of Graemie. When he reached the level he started running. Graemie looked down once. Then he was up there running bent forward against the rain.

We weren't going today, I knew. I didn't have to hide in the back now. However Madrid had gone up he wouldn't come down. Not in time. I believed in the action happening less than ever, if I had ever really believed it would. I would have to be in it from now on. If ever.

I sat back and finished my cigarette. I was tired. I could crawl into the back seat and be asleep in a minute. In the front. The car smelled smoky and damp. I listened to the radio and the rain, heavy on her. The dirt from Mexico was long washed off now. I was getting the warm feeling that comes when you're past feeling tired.

The music on the radio faded. An announcer came on. The weather bureau had phoned in the word . . . it was the latest. The rain would stop by tonight. It would be clear tomorrow and through the weekend. You could count on the parade and the rodeo Saturday in Cuesta. The Fiesta Day visitors would not be disappointed.

I rolled down the window and spit. I gave it all up, then. We were jinxed. That was it, all right. It had been today or nothing. I leaned back and shut my eyes.

There was more . . . another news bulletin. I brought my head up. I listened, feeling my neck tightening.

My cigarette burned my fingers, sticking to them. I grabbed the handle and hit the door with my shoulder. The radio was still going and I was running up the hill. I stopped to roll my cuffs up, then I didn't. I kept going.

Madrid's Plymouth was facing the slab of the burned-out house. Sand-o was leaning against the door on the driver's side. Graemie was standing by him. They saw me come up running. I signaled to them. They came away from Madrid's car, toward me.

I told them: why Madrid had driven up here, why he'd had to get his car off the road. Sand-o went white. Graemie looked away from me.

Madrid was getting out of the Plymouth. He didn't shut the door. He was in uniform and wearing his gun. He came over, bareheaded, the rain running down his face and spotting his shirt and trousers. He stopped a few yards short of us. Sand-o and Graemie turned toward him.

"We won't be looking at the bank today, hombre," he said to me.

He stood there, squat and unshaved, tired-looking, his uniform spoiling on him.

"She won't go with you, hombre," he said to me. "I made a mistake. I didn't think it would happen."

I slipped the middle button on my raincoat. Sand-o came for me. I hit his hands off and backed away. I reached inside the fly of my raincoat and pulled the .38 from my belt.

Sand-o said, "We'll get the chair!" He backed up from me, then started running. I didn't take my eyes off Madrid.

Graemie took a step. "Nick," he said, looking at Madrid.

Madrid's arms were at his sides. I couldn't tell if he was squinting against the rain, or what. He didn't move for his gun, that he had killed Lona with.

I shot him twice. I was aiming for him again on the ground, but Graemie ran into me.

NINETEEN

I pushed Graemie away. Madrid was lying on his side, his arm stretched out past his head. His hand was opening and closing. I went over, looking at him. He put his hand on the ground and tried to push with it in the mud. It must have hurt him and he stopped. The side of his face was on the ground, his eyes closed. Then the fingers of his outstretched hand uncurled, going limp. He went loose around the mouth. I watched but he looked gone, not moving. The rain even seemed to pour harder on him.

I looked at Graemie next to me.

"Stash the piece away, Nick."

I put it in my raincoat pocket. Then I took it out and put it in my belt.

"Our water's on, Nick."

"Mine is," I told him. Graemie boy.

"Ours, Nick. It's boiling."

"I—" But I shook my head. I didn't know what I was going to say.

"We better split out of here, hombre."

I looked around. Sand-o was already going down the hill. He might take the car, I thought, first. He might try to do it. The keys were in it.

It must have occurred to Graemie, maybe, at the same moment. He began running.

Sand-o had a start on us. I went down the hill behind Graemie. I slipped, hit on my knee, and got up.

Sand-o was getting in, on the driver's side. I reached the bottom of the hill and jumped the water in the gully. She turned over and the headlights came on. I ran around the driver's side and pulled the door open.

"Christ," Sand-o said, "what did you shoot him for?"

I couldn't talk. Graemie had the other door open.

I got my breath. "You were cutting out."

"Who was?"

"The hell. Get away from the wheel."

"We got to go!"

"I'll drive her." He shoved over and I got in.

"Where we going? Where can we go?"

"Shut *up*," I said. "What time is it—" I pulled back my sleeve. It was eighteen of three. I gunned the motor unconsciously.

"What can we do now? You killed a *heat!*"

"What kind of heat?"

"He *was* one."

"Give me a cigarette," I said.

"Give you *crut*."

"Here," Graemie said to me.

"F— you," I told Sand-o.

"Sure, *me. Sure.*"

The dash lighter popped and I dropped it. I touched the element picking it up. "Easy," Graemie said. I plugged back the lighter but Graemie held out a match.

A car came from behind, going past slow, and we looked at it.

"There's still time to get in the bank," I said.

"You fixed that too," Sand-o said.

"How?"

"What did you *shoot* him for? What did *that* do?"

"How's it fix the bank?"

"It fixes it."

"Listen," I said. "We'll all make the chair, all right. You can blame me, but it won't do you much good.

But we've got one chance. Turn this radio—" I cut the switch. "We have to get money, and get to Mexico. For a starter. And not tomorrow. That won't come."

They didn't answer. Either of them.

"Can we get there, Nick?" Graemie said.

"I'll get us. Right now."

"Let's do it. We have to do it."

"If you're out," I said to Sand-o, "get out. Here. I can't help it." But we couldn't go without him. Two couldn't do it.

He held still a second. I started to say, then he said: "Get us there."

I had her rolling.

We went down the Pass. I ran out of second gear but stayed in it around a couple of the hairpin turns. When we came to the sweeping ones I went into high. She swayed on me and I told Sand-o to brace himself more to stop crowding me.

Over the motor noise I asked him what he'd been talking about up there. I kept my eyes on the road. We were out of the Pass and moving. I had to lean toward him to hear him.

"I can't hear you."

"God *damn* it. He asked if we saw that item in the paper, right off. I played dumb and let him run through it. He was scared the kid—what was his name—"

"De la O." They'd had that part first on the radio.

"—would cop out on him. He said the kid pulled the Davidson's job on his shift—he set it up for him. He dry-backed him over here from Santa Lucia, in the trunk of his car, two months ago. It was the same kind of deal he was giving us—the protection stuff. The stuff he gave you to fence *was* from that Davidson's. So I was wrong."

"Slow up," I said. He was talking fast.

"You hear me?"

"Yes."

"I said I was wrong."

"Go ahead."

"Then he lost track of the kid. The kid kept pulling jobs, but he couldn't run him down. He was going to catch him and dump him back in Santa Lucia. The kid got half that Davidson's loot, that was all their deal called for. He had the rest of his stashed away in a place. He was scared to peddle it with that kid running loose and hot. The car the kid was driving was hot. The heat made the license number from their sheet."

"Yeah, so go on."

"So, then he told me he wanted us to clear out and go back, forget our deal. I was beefing with him when you came up. I thought he was just trying to get me to twist his arm—and the time was going. I thought he was making it all up to go with the story in the paper, just in case we had seen it. So I guess I was wrong."

The rain was blowing against the windshield, racing the wipers. "I was the first one wrong on him," I said.

"When he saw you he was surprised. But he didn't sound about it. He said was there a radio in the car. Then he said you probably had something."

"Where was he all morning?"

"Driving around, with his radio on, if the kid talked. Then he made up his mind to go home, give himself up from there. He figured the kid had to cop out, because the kid was a hype: When he'd start to need the stuff. But when he got to the house he didn't want to—tell Lona. He must have got there right after you talked to her. Then he came out to meet us and tell us the play was off. He figured he owed it to us. That's all he told me."

He had been on the square with us. He wasn't intending to double-cross us. But it meant nothing now.

"He was an addict himself," I said.

"*What? No.* He *wasn't.*"

"On the radio. The kid said so."

"You're scamming. What do you *know.* Then—" He swung toward Graemie. "You *knew* it."

Graemie rubbed his nose, sitting forward. He pulled the brim of his rain hat.

"Lona knew," I said. Graemie looked back at me.

I jerked my arm, uncovering my watch. It was eleven to three. I went out to pass a car. I took two of them.

"That's what the Davidson's job was for, then."

"Being down on the force, too," I said, "helped him do it."

"He must have been hooked."

"He had to quit the force before they picked up on him. He had to have more money, anyhow. So he picked out a bank, for a one-shot. Then he'd be through. He could sit still for a long while in Mexico." He just intended to take Lona with him, I thought. That was all. "That's the way it was," I said.

"We wouldn't have gone into it. Not if we knew he was a hype." He turned to Graemie.

Graemie looked out at me, past him. I studied the road.

"Don't put it on Lona, Nick," he said. "Maybe she turned him on—but she couldn't tell you. Because she was going to leave him. But I wouldn't have copped out on him. You—don't do it."

"We're not users," I said.

"You don't dig—" Graemie hesitated. "The way an—addict's—thinking." He didn't say more. He sat back.

"We would have been here, probably," I said. "Where we are now."

"Yeah," I thought Sand-o said. Maybe he grunted. I glanced at him. He scratched the wiry bristles on his face. They weren't beginning to be silky yet.

TWENTY

We were coming into town on the lower road off the Pass. The main drag was a few blocks to the left, and when the church steeples came in line, I turned up to it. There was no traffic to mention and two of the intersections were washed out. I went through the water without slowing. Then I made the turn into the square.

Some stores had their window lights on. But it had been getting lighter, I thought. The rain was still heavy, though. I overshot the driveway of the bank's parking lot; seeing I couldn't make it as I started turning, then straightening out because the brakes wouldn't hold. I backed up into my exhaust smoke after starting her and swung into the lot.

I backed up until I touched the wooden buffer. A scattering of cars were parked around. It was five of three. I got out and reached the suitcase from the floor in back. Sand-o got out after Graemie. Graemie moved in and slid behind the wheel.

"Pump the brakes," I told him, to dry them. He could see anyone coming out of the bank's front entrance. He couldn't see the doorway, but the sidewalk in front. "When we come out you'll have her running," I said. He made a circle with his thumb and finger. He'd taken care of himself, just a chippy one, before we'd left the motel. He was still all right with me.

I hurried across the lot with Sand-o. We walked under the sidewalk arch, and turned into the bank's entrance alcove. The guard was behind one of the doors. Sand-o leaned against the other, and I followed him inside.

We've made it, I thought. We're here. Sand-o slowed up and I almost bumped into him.

We knew the inside from Madrid's drawing. There were the officers' desks on the left through a gate, the teller windows after them in a line, then the vault. The teller windows were the old style with the brass bars. The writing tables were against the other wall. There were the big gold-framed paintings of early West scenes, one above each of the six marble topped tables. I glanced at one of a covered wagon and the team pulling it. A stand with a loan advertisement was in the middle of the floor, that Sand-o just missed hitting with his shoulder. We walked under the three big chandeliers hanging from the ceiling.

There were small chandeliers on long chains between the teller windows and the bookkeeping machines behind them. The tellers had fluorescent lights over their counters, and the girl machine operators, little lamps. The light from the plate glass windows over them wasn't much. I wished it were dark inside.

A few people were doing business at the teller windows. There were about fifteen employees in the place, and the same number of customers. Then Sand-o started going down the stairs next to the vault. We turned left, went through the washroom door, and we were under the vault. A fellow wearing a clerk's coat was at one of the sinks.

Sand-o went into the booth by the wall and slid the bolt on the door. I put the suitcase on the floor. I straightened up like when you kick at a ball and miss. It weighed nothing empty, but upstairs I had carried it pretty heavy-feeling. I ran the water in the sink and hit the soap container.

The clerk looked at me in the mirror. He was combing his hair, twisting a little curl in front. He ran hot water on his comb and I smelled the celluloid. Then he pushed the knob on the machine next to his mirror. I started at the noise. It was a hot-air blower. He ran a finger over his comb's teeth, making a sound that had the same effect on me as scraping a fork or cracking fingers. Then he went out.

The doorstop hissed, shutting.

I rubbed my hands under the blower. I looked down and saw the mud stains on my raincoat where I'd fallen.

"We're in the right place," Sand-o said behind the door.

"Open up."

He unlocked it, staying inside. "I'm scared that way."

"So am I."

He opened his trench coat and worked the .45 automatic out of his belt. He had it cinched there tight. I was ready to face the sink if anyone came in. I could see Sand-o in the mirror. He took off his rain hat and slapped it against the side of the booth.

"How long you think we'll have to wait for that guard?"

He was looking to me. I was cueing us the way it turned out.

"He didn't miss us coming down here."

When the guard came to roust us, I would be playing sick over the sink. Sand-o would have him covered, opening the booth door. The guard would see Sand-o's .45, looking down the barrel, or in the mirror. Sand-o had taken it because it was a big piece. We'd thought about cutting one of the rifles to fit inside the suitcase, but Sand-o didn't want to do it.

We didn't talk, then. We could hear our breathing, with the tile and quiet. I heard the plumbing go in the women's place on the other side of the stairway. Up above, on the street, we heard a siren going away. Sand-o cleared his throat. It was an ambulance siren.

The house isn't far from here, I thought. I don't know if I'd realized I would never see or talk to Lona again. Probably not yet.

It was three-ten, now. Maybe that old man, the guard, didn't like to make those stairs. Or he hadn't seen us coming down. Still, we'd figured he would check in here.

I was leaning against the sink, looking inside there at Sand-o. He had the lid down, sitting on it, holding back the door with his knee. I thought it probably was the first case of anyone's going inside one of those booths with a .45 in his hand. I would I have said it but he looked bad, too.

I was beginning to feel a little mean. It had come on me, suddenly, maybe thinking about Lona out at the house. Maybe it was seeing Sand-o, worried and uneasy in there, and I wanted to feel the difference. I wanted a cigarette too.

"Want to go up?" I said.

"Let's wait for the guard." He passed the .45 to his other hand, holding it flat.

He won't go through with it. If the guard comes he'll stay in there, I was thinking. He won't come out. I thought, look at him. He's almost forgetting what will happen if we don't go through with it, then make it to Mexico. Because they'll tie us to Madrid in a day or two. Maybe he thinks he won't draw the limit, he'll just get a few years because he didn't do it. He might even be thinking of turning me in, trying for a deal for himself. No. The hell no. He just has to raise that .45. And I've had it.

But the chair was there for me. It always would be.

I said, "They might be finding him up there. Then they'll block off the roads. We'll go up and I'll take the guard." It was the alternative we'd planned if the guard didn't come down.

Hell. What was hiding in a men's room anyway? "Wait five minutes more."

"Stay here. Don't come up chicken on me."

"I'm not chicken, damn it."

"I didn't think you were."

I picked up the suitcase. I unbuttoned the middle of my raincoat and my coat underneath. I put my hand in and touched the butt of the .38. I walked to the door.

"Wait." He squinted over the side of the booth. I let the door shut on him.

I got on the steps. I went up, came to the top, and stopped. I took the layout in quickly.

No customers were left on the floor. I saw the guard, then, at the side door. It was good; if he'd been up front I'd have had to walk him back. The shades were pulled down on the front doors, where we would be going out. I had to remember to get the key off him.

I stood on the top step for a moment, waiting. I tried to be cool. I might have to go down and pull that goddamn Sand-o out. Then I heard the washroom door tap. I looked down and he was on the steps. I wondered if I looked that bad. He had his hands in the pockets of his trench coat, his shoulders hunched; the one looking always a little higher than the other. His coat belt was hanging from the side loops.

The teller at the end window glanced over at me. I looked away from him. I started walking down the aisle toward the side door. No one was outside the vault, behind the marble railing. I passed the big round steel door. A man in a blue suit was inside the vault. He was wearing a white flower.

I figured Sand-o had crossed the aisle now and was going toward the desks up front. He had to go through the gate and throw down on the officers. Then he could see down the aisle between the tellers and the bookkeepers. He had to work fast, but it was all open up there. There was a chance he would have to blow a whistle on someone. He wasn't going to hit anyone but shoot over them. I hoped he was on his toes.

The guard saw me coming. I had to take his piece off him, then send him ahead of me, through the gate at my end. Then we'd have control except for the vault. If the guy didn't come out I'd put a shot in there.

The guard turned his back to me, working his key in the door. I smelled the rain as he pushed it open.

"Nick. Nick."

Sand-o was in back of me. He was on his toes all right; walking on them.

"You *son-of-a-bitch*," I said under my breath. These wasn't time now for him to get up front.

"Go in there." I jerked my head at the back gate.

I had the .38 out and turned around. The guard saw it. I pulled the hammer back for him, walking at him. His mouth opened, and he let the door shut.

Sand-o's boots scraped behind me, the gate buzzing as he went through it. I hurried toward the guard. Sand-o shouted, "This is a holdup!" it sounding loud as hell. Those bookkeeping machines stopped their clattering. I thought Jesus Christ if one of those officers has a gun up front that damn Sand-o.

Outside the door, a truck stopped. I saw it, gray-painted, through the glass, and the gun ports. And we were in the action—committed. It was like a dream, what Sand-o'd said Madrid would have waiting for us.

"Sand-o!" I yelled. "Back out!"

The guard heard the truck's cab door slam and went for his gun. I had to take him anyhow. I shot him almost holding the .38 in his stomach. I shook at the report it made inside. He went back, hitting against the door, tugging at his gun. I shot him through the head and he slid knee-bending down the glass. A big murmuring was behind me. I was still holding the suitcase and I dropped it. Then there began to be shouting and screaming.

The driver was coming around the front of the armored truck. A car stopped behind him, then got out of there. I shot at the driver through the glass as it spider-webbed near me. I hit the door, but it wouldn't budge. Then I turned the key in the lock. I slammed it open and heard the noise and the rain on the street.

Sand-o was in back of me shouting Nick Christ. I was outside and squeezed at the driver. He stood in the street shooting straight-armed at me in his uniform and cap. Sand-o's .45 went off in my ear, banging, then the driver turned sideways and fell on his face.

Someone was firing from inside the truck. They had a rifle sticking out of a side port. It went again, sounding like a rug being hit with a stick. I saw the guy's face through the rain in the little glass window above the barrel. I ran out into the street.

Sand-o was hit, holding his side with his bad arm.

He fired at the truck, the .45 slugs whanging off its steel side. I was around the front but I couldn't stop the gunner inside. Then Sand-o started running along the sidewalk, past the truck, and I froze inside. You couldn't yell at him. He was crouched over, his hat gone, his coat belt flapping. There was a horn blowing somewhere. I saw a guy running back up the sidewalk to the corner.

The guy in the truck shot behind Sand-o, taking a chunk of stucco out of the bank's wall. Then, shooting fast, he hit one of those big plate glass bank windows and it came crashing out like the end of something. Then I saw my car coming down the street, weaving around the cars whose drivers had let them, and Graemie blowing the horn, and I caught a glimpse of people holed up in doorways. Sand-o swerved, crossing the sidewalk for Graemie, then that shotgun went out of the side slot. It banged twice from the back of the truck, thudding, and Sand-o lifted in stride, still running bending over, the charges half-throwing him in front of my car.

I waited for Graemie now coming down a clear spot in the street. Turned on, straight, he was one cool head now, above the action. He couldn't have missed hitting Sand-o. The windshield blew out on one side but he came on. *Graemie boy*, he wouldn't stop. Then I saw he wouldn't stop.

I caught the door handle running. I saw Graemie behind the wheel, his face red all over like paint, and I walloped the side hanging on, but couldn't stay. I felt my leg twist out under me, then tried to get my hand out in front of my face before the street.

I could see Graemie still racing down the block. I heard him gun her, downshifting for that S-turn onto the street that led to the border road, but I knew Mexico. She fishtailed on the wet asphalt, overpowering like that. The spotlights came red, that was wrong too, and she went over. She rolled twice, flipping, straight on; then stayed on her top, turning half once around.

I watched the crowd coming out of nowhere to her. My leg wouldn't move and I couldn't get my head up. I wondered if the guy in the truck had enough angle to shoot at me if he would. I tried to swallow but my teeth felt like they were run up into the roof of my mouth. I heard shouting and the rain was like some thin curtain with things moving behind it but still hard to see.

I was thinking the best luck I could have was to go out.

If you read the papers in the beginning, it was a sort of mystery for a couple of days. Nobody knew the connection when they came down from Rialto Pass. That had to wait on me. The bank guard made it, and then finally the armored truck driver. He was here, on another floor, but he went after a few days. So they came to me. All that killing, they said. Long-faced. How do you feel about it now? They weren't thinking about Graemie, or Sand-o, you knew. How were you supposed to feel, I said; how did it happen he was crazy about Mexicans so suddenly? I asked this lieutenant. (He was one of my men, he'd said.) *Listen, you*, I'm coming up north and watch you get it. There were some reporters around then. The way it turned out, all right, we ran a better first to Fiesta Day than if we had come out.

They've got me on their security floor here. My jaw

is wired, and I think there's pins in it, too, like my leg. I can see the break in my leg with the light on and it's always on, through the window that's built in the cast. One of the hospital guards here understands I can't get to sleep too soon, this way. So he passes cigarettes to me. I've got half a pack, and one going now; I haven't set fire to the bed yet. It's not too bad, when I can smoke.

Except I keep going back. And there's no sense to it. Maybe, though, when there's nothing ahead. I even go over some things that happened years ago. Maybe, nothing things. When everybody was all even still in school.

Like coming away from a party, or show. And Lona going in the house to pick up her Levis. And I'd park down the block with the lights out, waiting, then watch her come out and get the porch light. We would drive over to the beach and sit on the sand, up front. Nobody would be out there, and you could hear the quiet there is just before the waves break. On the light nights your shadow was behind you if you turned. And I'd lay back with Lona, after a while, but not be able to look long, closely, at her. Or I would get the feeling we really wouldn't last.

Ahead of me, there's just my transfer coming up. We'll get on the road in two cars and run back to L. A. Then I'll take the train north to San Quentin. I won't get any good out of that; and not entirely the way you might think. I just never saw what that ever settled, or stopped. But I wouldn't want it that other way, either. Because I've been in here three weeks now and they don't seem like yesterday.

How long has it been, even, since we were sitting there in the back of Louis', and Louis looked in the

door and said, "A friend of yours outside, Nick." And I
said to him, "I thought you knew all my friends." And
Louis said, "Do you have any left?"

But that Louis never knew what he was saying.

THE END

CHARACTER-ISMS

BALL—to make love
BEAST, BOMB—hotrod
BLOW THE WHISTLE ON, SNAP OFF AT—to shoot
BUST, BUSTED—to arrest, be arrested
CHIPPY ON—to cheat on
CLUE YOU—to tell you, let you know
CONNECTION, PUSHER—narcotics peddler
COP OUT—to squeal, to back out of a responsibility
CRUT—shit
DEEJAY—disk jockey
DINGIE—crazy, psychotic
FUZZ, HEAT—cop, cops
GEORGE—O.K., fine
GIG—job
GOOF, GOOFING—to take drugs, be on drugs; also, to
   fail, make a mistake
GRASS, JIVE, MARYJANE, POD—marijuana
HARD STUFF, HORSE—heroin
HIP—aware, in the know
HYPE—drug addict
JOINT, ROACH, COCKTAIL—reefer; diminishing sizes
JUNK, JUNKIE—morphine, morphine (or drug) addict
LUSH, LUSHED—drink, to be drunk
NARCO HEAT—Bureau of Narcotics agent
PIECE—gun
SCAM, TO SCAM—phony, lying, to lie
SCENE—situation
SCORE—to buy narcotics
SPIKE—needle for a fix
STOMP INTO, CHARGE—to hold up, rob
STRAIGHT, SWINGING, TURNED ON—to be high on
   drugs
THROW DOWN ON—to pull a gun on
TOKE—to inhale on, smoke, a reefer
TOM—sad, bad
TOTAL—to knock out, finish off, kill
TURN TRICKS—to engage in prostitution
WHITE STUFF—cocaine

Black Gat Books

9 798886 011364